THE CHAINS THAT BIND

BOOK 3: THE RUNESPELL SERIES

SARAH BUHRMAN

Black Rose Writing | Texas

First printing

This is a work of fiction. Names, characters, businesses, places, events, and incidents are either the products of the author's imagination or used in a fictitious manner. Any resemblance to actual persons, living or dead, or actual events is purely coincidental.

ISBN: 978-1-68433-230-4
PUBLISHED BY BLACK ROSE WRITING
www.blackrosewriting.com

Printed in the United States of America
Suggested Retail Price (SRP) $16.95

The Chains that Bind is printed in Adobe Caslon Pro

This book is dedicated to my husband, who has continued to support me in this endeavor, and to Tamara, my VPA and second-best supporter. I would also like to thank my parents for occasionally taking the kids, the kids for occasionally behaving well, and Marketta Sowers, who edited in a rather small timeframe.

THE CHAINS
THAT BIND

CHAPT 1

"Are you still having nightmares?"

"Every night," I sighed. I avoided looking the shrink. She had the kind of eyes that saw straight through words and pried out the ugly truth. I was definitely avoiding that.

"Have you been meditating every day?" she asked.

I squirmed. "I'm trying," I said, frowning at the whine in my voice. "I just can't seem to stay focused."

Dr. Walters nodded, the ends of her hair waving a bit at the movement. I stared at the mahogany cloud, fascinated.

Dr. Yolanda Walters was a lovely woman, about 10 years my senior who radiated calm. I liked her. I liked her easy smile, the way her very white teeth gleamed against the dark tones of her lips and gums. I liked the way her hair billowed out from her head in waves of reddish-brown that defied gravity and entranced me.

After three tries to find a psychologist I could work with, Dr. Walters' progressive style and non-judgmental aura was just what I needed. She reminded me of Kaitlyn, the woman who was one of the few points of stability at the Center. She reminded me of Yamaya, too. After encountering the African goddess in a vision, she had come to represent the kind of strength and support I needed to get through this emotional fall-out.

"It's common for people to have difficulty concentrating or staying on task," the doctor said.

"I'm jumpy," I blurted out. "In more ways than one."

The doctor nodded and waited for me to continue.

"Like, I get so nervous with sudden sounds," I explained. "Especially ones that sound like water splashing." I shivered. "And crowds. I feel like a long-tailed cat in crowds, just waiting for someone to do something that hurts me."

Dr. Walters made some notes, nodding.

"But I'm also constantly changing what I'm doing," I said. "I'll be filling orders, and I'll jump up and start supper. Only it's like two in the afternoon. So I'll go clean the girls' room. Then halfway through that, I'll remember I need to pick up the mail." I shook my head. "It takes me twice as long to get anything done."

The woman across from me shot me a sympathetic look. "Nicola, I have to tell you, given what you'd been through, all of this is totally normal. Anxiety and loss of executive function are both extremely common reactions to the kind of trauma you've been through."

I snorted. "I can't afford to be normal if that means broken," I muttered.

Dr. Walters nodded her understanding. "It's frustrating, having to take the time to heal, having to deal with scars and," her eyes flickered down to my feet then back up to my face, "things that are gone."

I huffed out a wry laugh. "That's an understatement."

She leaned forward. "Nicola, I've seen a lot of people with these issues, and I have high hopes of you being able to overcome them. You are honest with yourself and incredibly self-aware."

I grimaced.

"But," she continued, "you need to let yourself feel what you feel. You need to dig out the fear and the anger and the pain, and let yourself feel them."

I opened my mouth, then realized I had nothing to say to that. I completely agreed with her even if I didn't want to do it.

"You don't have to do it all at once, though," Dr. Walters warned. "You have had a lot happen and trying to push it too fast could overwhelm you."

I slumped in the overstuffed chair. "I'm overwhelmed every day of my life," I said.

"With two kids and an at-home business," she said, "I can imagine you are. Perhaps you should take some time off."

I shrugged my shoulders. "Well, Joseph - my friend from Indie - he's been trying to get me to go on some hiking trip with him," I said. "Do you think that would be wise, though? I thought I was supposed to be getting my life together, not traipsing off to go on long walks."

Dr. Walters grinned. "Vacations are a part of life, Nicola. We need to rest and get out of our routines just as much as we need to have our routines to begin with." She jotted a few more notes and closed the notebook. "As your doctor, I suggest you consider this trip. It might be just what you need to get past this plateau in your progress."

I grimaced. "Okay, I guess. What's the worst that could happen?"

• • •

I sat back on the sofa, my feet propped up on the coffee table. Ella and Maria sprawled on a tangled pile of blankets and pillows on the floor. Tiny snores floated up from them both. At 9 and 8, they were still young enough to enjoy camping on the floor and, despite their best efforts, they still didn't have the staying power to make it until midnight.

I stared at the TV, telling myself it was time for bed. Instead, I pointed the remote at the screen and played another movie I'd seen a million times on the streaming service. I sighed and struggled to keep my eyes open. It wasn't that I had to stay awake. I just didn't want to face the images in my head, and they always came out when I slept.

I yawned so hard, my jaw popped. I reached over to grab my cup of tea only to find it was empty. I sighed and let my head fall back to rest on the back of the sofa. I pulled out my phone and brought up my favorite social media app. It only took a few minutes of tapping and scanning to realize there wasn't anything there to distract me from my exhaustion.

I sent a message to Joseph, asking about some detail of our trip that we'd already covered a hundred times. I stared at the message, hoping the little dots would appear to let me know he was responding. Finally, I let my hand fall to my side. Despite my efforts to stay awake, my eyes closed to the sound of a princess singing about fitting in.

• • •

"I still can't believe I let you talk me into this."

Joseph glanced over at me from the other side of the back seat. The driver ignored us. He'd been paid to drop us off at a specific location, and we had not encouraged small talk, so he had the radio on low and seemed content to hum along with the alt-rock station.

"You needed a break," Joseph said. "The online business, two kids, your mother. And you never really got a chance to recover from that crap last year. Or the year before."

I shrugged. "It all worked out."

Joseph snorted. "You need a vacay, so that's what you are getting."

"Yeah, but hiking?" I smirked. "I like nature and all, but I also like room service, massages and central air."

"The Appalachian Trail is one of the greatest nature excursions in the world. A few days hiking through New Hampshire to Maine will give us the opportunity to camp in the most gorgeous forests on the planet."

The grin froze on my face. "Wait. Camping? You didn't say anything about camping. At night. Outside."

Cold, numbness began to creep along my cheeks, and I struggled to keep my breathing even.

Joseph patted my hand, his eyes on the scenery flicking by while he watched for our turnoff. "It's June. Even this far north it only gets down to the upper 50s." He shot a glance at my face. "We won't freeze to death."

And just like that the world ended.

Featureless faces swam in my vision, covering Joseph's concerned expression as the Hands held me under the water. My breath came in gasps and ice flooded my veins like waves in the Arctic. My legs, back and arms tensed, every muscle clenching.

I felt a sharp pain in my toes, toes that were no longer there. I reached for the lava-rage deep inside, but the cold was too strong. Tears leaked from my eyes and my head felt full and empty at the same time, making me dizzy. My stomach heaved weakly, and I struggled not to vomit, thrash, scream, run...

"Nicola!"

Strong hands grasped my shoulders, shaking me gently. My head began to clear. I clutched at Joseph's arms and let him pull me into a firm hug, the pressure doing something to my autonomic nervous system that shorted out the panic response. At least a little bit.

Dr. Walters said I had PTSD, and I was being triggered. I'd heard of triggers before, and I'd been half sympathetic, half-frustrated by many of them. I'd had no idea.

It was literally as simple as Joseph saying "freeze to death," and the world was no longer safe, fun, exciting, or even just comfortable. It was the terror. It was the panic. It was the helplessness and the need for adrenaline-giving rage that just wouldn't come.

As the tension broke, I bawled in Joseph's arms.

CHAPT 2

I walked behind Joseph, thumbs tucked into the straps of my backpack. He had intentionally chosen a stretch of the trail that was easy to hike and beautiful to see. The dense trees created a dome of green that filtered the sun's rays into a kind of verdant glow.

Even though I knew that the plant-life along the trail was full of variety and a rich, living habitat, I found myself in awe over the shapes of leaves, the shades of green. Each breath brought a scent of earth and chlorophyll, full of humidity and high oxygen levels that left me slightly dizzy if I breathed too deeply for too long. Each step showed branches swaying in breezes or from movement in the underbrush.

The trail was well marked, a worn path with traces of mulch. So many hikers used the trail that it was a matter of safety to have some maintenance over it. Still, nature prevails, and the edges of the trail were filled with saplings, bushes, ferns and grasses, all pushing up to get their fair share of the filtered light.

Winds blew through the tops of the trees above us, and the rustling leaves made a kind of rushing roaring sound, like a waterfall or pouring rain. Squirrels and rabbits occasionally stared at us from their spots, frozen in the brush and convinced they hadn't been seen. Birds chirped and tweeted all around, but I only saw a few of those, and I couldn't identify most of them anyway.

It was a lesson in how little I'd connected to nature lately. Like so many, I got caught up in life, taking care of Ella, and now Maria, working on my business, shopping for groceries, and paying the bills.

And on Tuesdays and Thursdays, I went to therapy. Maria went to therapy on Thursdays as well, dealing with her own issues. I tried not to let my pain become her burden, too.

I was lucky to have found a therapist who didn't criticize my religious choices, but it was hard to explain the full extent of what had happened. I told Dr. Summers that I didn't know what Zaro had used on us. I just explained the effects. She assumed it was Ecstasy. I also had a hard time explaining why I'd joined the Hands in the first place, but my fumbled attempts to do so seemed to convince her that I'd just been lonely, an easy target.

Despite those sticky issues, I kept going because when I told her the basics of what had happened, she hadn't given me platitudes or tried to make me feel like I should have done better. Instead, she talked about how hard it was to deal with the complexities and asked about details with compassion.

I spent a lot of time crying in therapy. It was about the only time I let those walls down, especially with two observant girls in the house.

I just couldn't explain to anyone else what I felt. Not my mother, not Joseph. How could they ever understand that I felt guilty about all of it? I should have stopped them sooner. I should have seen the patterns. I should have been able to overcome the diet and the monotony and the power of the Runespell. I should have been able to fight Nancy. I should have been able to face Bob. I should have stopped Zaro from touching me, and worse.

How could I show them how broken I was? How could I let them know that I sometimes regretted beating Zaro? How could I tell them I still wanted that horrible, wonderful, will-destroying Touch?

I stared at the solar charger perched on the shoulder strap of Joseph's back as he moved around a winding part of the trail. A long black cord coiled up and into one of the side pockets, charging his phone as he walked. I thought about what Joseph might say if I told him that I still, after nearly a year, tried to use the First Runespell on myself.

I jerked my hand away from the pendants lying warm on my chest under my shirt. Five pendants out of six, the Runespells that I'd nearly died to collect. Nearly died, twice. Actually died, once.

I couldn't even bring myself to tell Joseph that I had given the Second Runespell away, entrusted to the Norns, who had supposedly given it to a person who had certain gifts that would help them deal with the crushing moral dilemma that would eventually wear away anyone who used it.

I worried about that, too. It wasn't that I thought I'd be able to handle the Runespell. It had taken all of a few seconds after realization hit to know that I would go insane trying to work with the consequences of that particular power. Ironically, not many could just heal the sick without shredding their own compassion to pieces.

I blinked, stumbling to a halt as I realized Joseph had stopped by the trail, looking into the trees. I noticed a smaller footpath going that way.

Joseph pointed. "This is one of the campsites I considered for this first night," he said. "We've made good time, but it would be a stretch to make it to the next site before dark. I think we should stop here."

I nodded. "Sounds good."

•   •   •

The campsite had a small cabin, an outhouse, and two fire pits. We had set up the tents after we realized a group of college students hiking from the other direction had already settled into the cabin. I braced myself for socializing with the strangers.

I stepped out of the tent and Joseph looked up from his place squatting in front of our small fire. He smiled and handed me a cup of something hot. I smelled it. Chicken and rice soup. Joseph and I settled on a large log and sipped at the warm liquid. An old-fashioned percolator sat on the coals, bubbling water into coffee for later.

Fortunately, the college students didn't seem to be too interested in much small talk. A few came over to say hi and ask about the condition of the trail we'd walked that day. They warned us about some muddy spots and a small clearing with a weasel-musk smell that we might want to avoid. Then they went to bed, complaining about having to make good time in the morning.

We sat on the ground with our backs to the log and our legs stretched out beside the fire. We sipped coffee and talked about our plans for the next few days' hikes.

"The coffee isn't going to be a daily thing," Joseph commented. "It'll be mostly tea. Coffee just isn't space efficient."

I nodded. I was glad he was talking about the plans and details, but I was even happier that I wasn't being expected to make decisions.

"We'll stop the day after tomorrow for more water and a few extras. The trail cuts through Norwich and Hanover at the border of Vermont to New

Hampshire so we can refresh all our supplies."

"Hmm," I said.

"Or we can give it up and go home," Joseph offered.

I looked up. I knew I was being less than enthusiastic about the whole thing, and Joseph's words held no anger or animosity. "No," I said. "I'm fine. It's just as beautiful and refreshing as you said." I shrugged my shoulders. "I just have to deal with this baggage, you know?"

He nodded. "Do you want to talk about it?"

I shook my head. "It's hard to admit this stuff. I can tell my therapist. That's her job. But I'd have to look you in the eye. It would be hard to do that, not because of you or anything you might do, but because of me." I sighed. "I don't know how to explain it. I need you to be separate from that stuff."

Joseph patted my hand. "I get it. I mean, not completely, but I kind of get it. It's like why I don't talk about Dan."

I nodded. Joseph's boyfriend had died in a car accident years ago. He never really talked about it, and I could understand why. It would be like reopening that wound every time.

"Nicola." A woman's voice rang out with a familiar confidence, and my heart sunk. The only women I knew who spoke and moved through the world like some kind of Amazon queens were...

A form stepped out of the forest, blonde hair and blue eyes shining in the firelight. Her practical clothing looked like any other hiker on the trail, but the bowie knife at her belt was as magical as she was. Valkyrie.

I glared up at the woman. "Rade, isn't it?"

Her head inclined. "Yes. You've been avoiding us, and we have allowed it. But it is time for you to learn to control your abilities."

I sighed and Joseph shot me a questioning look. "Joseph, Rade, one of the Valkyrie," I said. "She wants me to learn to embrace and use the Berserker rage."

Rade nodded. "It may come in handy in the future, just as it has been useful in the past."

I snorted. "In the past, I nearly killed someone."

Rade stared at me impassively. "In the future, nearly may not be good enough."

I turned my eyes away from the Valkyrie and saw Joseph, his gaze moving between Rade and myself. His expression was one of surprise and a little bit of shock and horror. I swallowed hard and wished my vacation had stayed a vacation.

CHAPT 3

I sat in the tent, shifting as my butt noticed rocks and sticks underneath the tent floor. I concentrated on laying out the sleeping pad and the sleeping bag on top of it. The bag was a pretty decent one, made for just the kinds of temperatures we could expect on this trip.

Joseph had done a good job, but my thoughts skittered away from focusing on actually sleeping outside in the slightly chilly night-time weather. It wasn't his fault. He couldn't have known that I still dreamt of shivering violently, of floating in ice water, of faces watching me as I slipped away. Nancy's face. Bob's face.

The blond man ducked into the tent and handed me a wool blanket. "I brought a couple of these, just in case," he said.

I took the blanket and glanced past it to his face. Guilt showed in the set of his mouth and the concern in his eyes. I forced a smile. "Thanks."

Joseph set up his own bedroll quickly, then sat and watched me fuss with mine. "I'm really sorry, Nicola," he murmured. "When I planned this, I didn't think about how it might... bring stuff back. I had no idea."

"I know." I shook my head wryly. "How could you? I never talked about it."

Joseph nodded. "But I knew about the tests, and I knew the stuff Z—"

I shot him a look, half anger, half panic. Joseph swallowed the name and cleared his throat.

"I know what that asshole did to you has stuck with you. I guess we all focused on that and ignored the fact that you..." He trailed off, his face going a few shades paler.

I watched him for a moment. "Died," I croaked out. "I died, and I have the missing body parts to prove it." I waggled my foot at him.

He flinched, and I bit my lip. I was taking my emotional distress out on him. Yeah, he was the reason I was experiencing it right now, but it wasn't really his fault. I had never really talked about dying.

I stared at the wool blanket in my hands, rubbing the nubby fabric between my thumb and forefinger. The silence stretched as I tried to force the words out. I screamed them in my head, but my lips stayed shut with my voice locked in my throat.

Joseph shifted as if to stand up, and I cursed myself for being a coward. The sudden flood of shame unlocked my words, and they tumbled over themselves to get out.

"I went astral before I died," I said.

Joseph froze. "What?"

"I was trying to get away from the dying. So I slipped into the astral plane. That's where I was when I was... not alive."

He frowned. "That shouldn't happen. How did you manage to focus in that kind of distress?"

I pursed my lips. There was another thing I'd more or less skimmed over in my retellings. "I had been going to the astral a lot. It was... kind of an addiction."

"Oh." Joseph's face remained carefully neutral, but I could still see it. Fear, confusion, disappointment. "That's not good."

"No, it wasn't," I sighed. "And when they brought me back, it yanked me out of the astral plane, violently. Almost physically." I rubbed my sternum where the heart-thread had torn my spirit from one realm into another.

"Ouch! That had to suck." Joseph watched my face for a moment until I ducked my head under his scrutiny. "So, why did you jump into the astral? Was there a lot of pain?"

I shrugged. "Not at the end," I said. "When I first got in the water... oh, gods, it was so cold. I couldn't stop my arms and legs from jerking because I was shivering so hard. I couldn't talk because my jaw was chattering and my neck was so tight I could barely breathe." I shuddered at the memory. "Then it just kind of faded away. And I don't remember much, just flashes and images."

"So why did you try to escape?" Joseph pressed gently.

I sucked on my lip, thinking. "I'm not entirely sure, but I think I knew I was going to die. I think I was afraid. For me, obviously, but also for Ella." I shrugged. "When I got to the astral, I had to let that go to shake off the shadow spirits."

"Oh, the Fears?" Joseph smiled at my look. "The shades that come and get you when you go in afraid. I call them Fears. Like, the only thing you have to fear is..." He waved his hand in a circle to imply the end of the phrase.

I barked a laugh. "That's really a perfect name for them. Fears." I nodded. I reached out to straighten the sleeping bag again. "It's weird, though."

"Oh?" Joseph asked.

I looked up at him. "I've died. I've faced death. When that happens, it's supposed to make death less... terrifying. You know, because we are just afraid of the unknown."

Joseph nodded.

I looked back down at the blanket. The nubby fabric blurred as my eyes filled with sudden tears. "But I'm more afraid of death than ever."

"I can see why." Joseph held up his hands at my look. "Bear with me, okay? You faced losing everything. That brings your whole world into a kind of crystal clarity, right? You knew, without a doubt, what was important to you. And you almost lost it."

"Yeah." I frowned, trying to figure out where he was going with this.

Joseph shrugged. "Dying and coming back didn't change that. You still find those things important. And, you can still lose them."

I nodded slowly. "I guess so."

Joseph stood up, bending over his pack for a moment. "It says a lot about you, though." He pulled out the pot and a can of stew. He pointed the stew at me. "Your priorities are solid, and you value your connections more than your things. Supper will be ready in about 10 minutes."

He ducked out of the tent and left me to consider his words.

●　　　●　　　●

"Again!"

I closed my eyes, letting my anger grow inside. I focused on the unfairness and the frustration over how much pressure the Valkyrie was putting on me.

The hot rage bubbled in my gut, and I pulled on it, encouraging it to come closer to the surface, to flow up past my heart and into my neck. The heat warmed my ears for a moment before...

Memories flashed behind my eyes. Maria crying, Kaitlyn watching me with wary eyes, Zaro's face as he stole my will and used my body. Zaro's face, bloody and shapeless under my fists. Nancy pressing her hand over my mouth, Bob staring with one eye from the wrappings over his head. The Hands watching me, kind and hopeful, faces wavering through the water...

Icy cold splashed through my arms, flowing into my chest. My heart stuttered, tripping over its beat. The lava cooled instantly, anger retreated from the fear. The power of the rage was quenched with a jolt.

I opened my eyes, bent over with my hands braced on my knees. My breath came in panting gasps.

"Why do you keep failing? Why do you let your fear overcome you?"

I looked up at Rade. Her eyes were the bright blue of glaciers and just as kind.

I pushed myself up, feeling a weakness in every muscle down to my bones. "I don't know," I muttered. "You're the expert."

Rade scowled. "I can tell you how it is done, but I can't do it for you."

My temper flared. Not the rage I'd been struggling with for the past hour, but just a regular snarky bite of anger. "And I can tell you what's going on with me, but I can't understand it for you. Do you even have compassion?"

Rade stared at me. "No, it is not part of my duties to have that kind of connection to mortals."

I snorted. "Maybe we should get Mercy here—"

"Mercy will not come," Rade cut in. "By her choice."

I frowned. "She doesn't want to help?"

Rade shook her head. "She believes that her presence, while comforting, will not help with what you need," Rade sighed, annoyance written on her face. "She suggested I be the one to do this."

"You don't seem too happy with that," I pointed out.

"I do what needs to be done," Rade said. "Regardless of my feelings on the matter."

"Okay, ladies," Joseph cut in, stepping through the trees to the small clearing where Rade had taken me to train. He ignored the dirty looks that both of us shot him. "Nicola and I need to get going or we are going to be behind in our timeline. Which means running out of food and water, for those in the peanut gallery who haven't been paying attention."

I sighed, trying to be irritated, but I was more than happy to end this exercise in emotional frustration. I waved to Rade and walked back towards our camp. I knew it was a bit rude and disrespectful, but my socializing energy was tapped out.

I found the camp packed up. Joseph had been keeping himself busy while I'd been caught up in the stupid useless exercises Rade had run me through. I slung my pack over my shoulders, staggering a bit when I underestimated the weight of the pack. I was headed to the trail when Joseph caught up.

"So, that went well, I gather?" he asked, humor coloring his words.

I snorted. "Valkyrie A.I. doesn't know what's wrong with me," I muttered.

Joseph kept pace while I stalked along the trail. "There's nothing wrong with you, Nicola," he said after a moment. "You've been through a lot, and she just doesn't get it."

"No shit, Sherlock," I growled.

Joseph laughed. "Come on, that's no reason to get childish about it." I could feel his eyes on my back. "Unless there's something to what she's saying."

I stalked up an incline, taking it too fast and slipping several times on wet grass and dew-slick clay as I huffed up the slope. I got to the top and waited for Joseph to catch up. I stared out at the trees, light filtering through the leaves.

Joseph moved up beside me, watching the trees without a word. He always seemed to know when I just needed some quiet to think.

"You're right," I mumbled. "She's right. Everyone is so damned right."

Joseph waited. I could feel the energy of his presence, energy of encouragement that he simply released for me, not at me, not forcing me to deal with it. It was just there for me. It warmed me.

"I can't stop the memories," I said. "I feel the rage, I can reach for it. But then the memories come."

I heaved a sigh. "The last time I called up the Berserker power, there was so much that had built up to it. I just can't separate that out."

I saw him nod out of the corner of my eye.

"You didn't have much practice with it before that to fall back on," he pointed out.

"Understatement," I bit out. "Before that, it was when I went all rage machine on a basement wall."

He nodded again. "Not exactly a great basis to build your experiences on."

I shrugged and turned down the trail. I set a more realistic pace, and Joseph walked beside me instead of letting me lead.

"I want to help you, Nicola," he said after a few minutes. "I know I don't know all the crap you're facing, but I want to help you."

I nodded. "I just have a hard time with the whole idea of you knowing. Because then I'd have to face you knowing that you know." I shook my head. "Gods, it's so complicated and..."

"Emotional," Joseph supplied. "So let's make a deal." I looked up at him with an eyebrow raised. "We can take turns. You reveal a secret, and I'll reveal a secret. If we want to ask a question, we have to seriously consider answering that same kind of question."

I stared at him for a moment. "Dan?" I asked.

He swallowed hard and nodded. I considered. Having someone know the icky dark secrets I held was one thing. Getting their icky dark secrets in return was... well, more equal. It took away whatever emotional advantage was inhibiting my ability to talk.

"Okay," I said. "I'll try."

CHAPT 4

I sat on the steps to the shelter and watched the group of people laughing. The firelight reflected off their faces as several of them told raunchy stories and jokes to keep us entertained. Joseph grinned at me from a few feet away, then turned back to the guy he was chatting up. Always more social than I was, he was in his element.

Once again, we found ourselves sharing a campsite with another group of hikers. This time, the four men had invited us to share the shelter with them. We declined the offer but accepted their invitation to hang out.

As we ate a supper of stew and bread, I noticed one of the guys kept glancing at me. He caught my eye and gave me a friendly smile. He seemed to be less enthused by the rowdiness of his friends, and I figured he was more like me and less gregarious than his companions. I returned his smile with a wry grin.

I finished my stew and twisted around to set my dishes on the floor behind me. When I turned back, the smiling guy was lowering himself onto the step beside me.

"Hey," he said.

"Hi." I nodded my head at the group as they burst into another round of loud laughter. "Your friends seem like a fun group."

He laughed. "Yeah, I guess." He reached over with his right hand. "I'm Jake."

I smiled and shook his hand. It was warm and dry. "Nicola," I offered.

"Do you hike the trail often?" Jake asked.

I shook my head. "First time, actually."

"Ah. How do you like it?"

"It's nice," I admitted. "Much better than I thought it would be."

Jake nodded. "It's gorgeous in the fall. There's this place a few miles south where the trees just burst with gold and red leaves." He grinned at me. "Too bad you won't be here for that. I'd love to show you."

I blushed. The man was flirting with me. Not that I minded, but it had been a while, and I wasn't used to it. I hadn't flirted much since breaking up with Keith...

I suppressed a shiver, pushing away the memories that threatened to surface. Jake noticed and grabbed a blanket from nearby, throwing it over my shoulders. His action startled me, and I jumped when he put his arm over my shoulders on top of the blanket. I realized he was trying to warm me up, but he hadn't given me any warning of what he was doing, and he came across as aggressive and overbearing because of that.

I shrugged my shoulders, trying to ignore my discomfort. The guy was nice, and I wouldn't mind getting to know him better. He had no idea he was making me nervous, and I wasn't sure how to explain it to him, or if I even wanted to bring it up.

"You must be chilly," Jake murmured, rubbing my arms through the blanket. "Not used to being this far north, I take it?"

I gave him a tight smile. "Yeah, it gets a bit colder here than in Indiana."

"That's where you're from?" Jake slipped his hand under the blanket, tracing his fingers along the inside of my arm. "Pretty far from home."

I closed my eyes. Part of me really wanted to enjoy the touch. It wasn't much, and I'd been mostly celibate since Ella was born. But it was the mostly that was the problem.

Jake's hand moved over my arm, but it was Zaro's touch that I felt in my mind. It was Zaro trying to whisper in my ear. It was Zaro crowding me, filling my head with images, sensations, feelings that stole my will and left me defenseless.

I could feel the Center's guru pressing me down on my back, hands at my thighs. It wasn't Jake whose lips pressed against mine, or whose hands held me pinned. I felt the familiar longing for the Touch of Peace that Zaro gave while taking his "wives," like the siren-song of a drug to an addict. At the same time, my stomach churned with hate and revulsion.

My skin pebbled with goosebumps as my memory brought back the feeling of ice water and terror. My heart galloped in my chest and my breath froze in my throat. I could hear the *thu-thump thu-thump* in my ears.

Zaro reached out and ran his hand up my arm. He reached for his neck and grasped the wire pendant with his right hand while stroking my face with his left. I felt a warmth rush through my body, like a blanket on a cold, winter day. My eyes went unfocused and my limbs fell limp. I'd never felt such peace. It enveloped me, shoving out any discomfort. Pushing away my will. Darkness flooded over me...

"Nicola! Nicola!"

I focused on Joseph's voice, calling me back from the horrors in my head. My eyes fluttered open, and I found myself flat on my back on the ground at the foot of the stairs to the shelter.

Joseph brushed hair from my face. "Nicola, can you hear me?"

I gulped and nodded. He helped me sit up and I glanced around, trying to get my bearings. Jake stood at my feet, staring with concern on his face. His friends stood around a few feet away, watching and shifting on their feet.

"Is she okay?" one of the guys called.

Joseph glanced over at the one who had spoken. "She'll be fine."

"What happened?" Jake asked in a shaky voice. "We were just talking and then she just..." He waved his hands as if that would describe it.

Joseph shook his head and frowned down at me. I looked away. I could feel my face pulling into the kind of frown you get before you start crying hard.

Joseph turned to Jake and his friends. "Seizures," he said. "She doesn't get them often, but the extra exercise must have been too much." He helped me to my feet. "I guess we'll head home tomorrow," he said to me.

I opened my mouth to protest before I realized that Joseph knew I didn't get seizures. He was making up a believable story so I wouldn't have to explain all my mental and emotional issues to a group of virtual strangers. I shot him a smile and let him guide me to the tent. I waited until we were out of earshot before looking up at him.

"Thanks."

He shrugged. "Yeah. Just, maybe tell me what happened?"

I nodded. "Can it wait 'til morning? I feel like I just ran a marathon and then got hit by a truck."

"Sure thing."

●　　●　　●

"So, when Dan was killed, I had nothing to be angry about," Joseph spoke quietly. "It was a total accident. It could have happened to anyone. I couldn't justify anger at anyone, so I just suppressed it."

I raised my eyebrows. "How'd that work out?"

Joseph laughed. "It didn't," he admitted. "I ended up severely depressed."

I opened my mouth.

"Nope," he cut me off. "It's your turn."

I blew out a breath, puffing up my cheeks. "I freeze up, literally," I said in a rush. "It's like I'm back there, reliving the whole situation. And I'm so afraid I won't be able to win this time."

I ducked my head and forced the words out before I could stop. "When Jake touched me, it was like I was back at the Center with that man—"

I snapped my mouth shut on the words. I stared at a crooked branch sticking out into the clearing. It looked a bit like the letter "L." I focused on the branch and continued. "The Berserker rage was so entwined with... with desperation that night. Now, all I can feel is the desperation. It suffocates me and makes me afraid. But I can't seem to bring rage up without that desperation now—"

"Interesting."

Rade's cold voice cut across the evening air. My head shot around, and I glared at her.

"You could try knocking, you know," I growled.

Rade slashed her hand across her body in a dismissive gesture. "No time," she said. "There is something you need to know."

Two large black birds landed between us, tilting their heads to the side in unison. I bit back a cry of joy and tried to get my features to show surprise instead of a grin.

"These are not normal ravens," Rade said, gesturing to the birds. "They are Odin's messengers, Huginn and Muninn."

"Really?" I said. I nearly choked when the reddish-black bird, Muninn, opened its mouth in a kind of laughing pantomime.

"Behave," Rade snapped at the birds. "Show them your other form."

The ravens exchanged a glance and shook themselves. As their feathers shivered over their bodies, their forms grew. In only a few seconds, the ravens stood up in their twin human forms. They were tall and thin with sharp features and shaggy, feathery black hair.

I clapped my hands over my mouth, covering up a giggle, but pretending to be in shock.

"Nicola!" Huginn cried, opening his arms to me.

"You remember us?" Muninn asked, mirroring Huginn's gesture.

"We brought Mercy," Huginn said.

"And sandwiches," Muninn offered.

I jumped up from my seat and walked towards the two, embracing them.

"Of course, my friends," I said. "But you are the ravens? Amazing!"

The twins' eyes glinted mischievously as they played along. "We had no need to say before," Muninn pointed out.

"You had other things to worry about," Huginn reminded me.

The smile slipped from my lips. "Yeah, I guess I did."

Rade cleared her throat. "The messengers have something for you," she prompted, scowling at the dark-haired young men.

I raised an eyebrow at her. "Is it a, uh… message?" I asked, trying to keep a straight face.

"Not really," said Huginn.

"Not directly," Muninn clarified. "You have a signal catcher."

"A what?" Joseph said. He'd moved up behind me.

"Ray-dee-oh," Huginn said, enunciating oddly, as if he'd never used the word before. "To catch the signals."

I nodded, and Joseph dug in his pack for the hand-crank radio. He turned the crank handle a dozen times and clicked it on. "What station?"

"No matter," Huginn said.

"It matters not," Muninn agreed.

Joseph shot me a glance and I shrugged. I held out my hand, and he passed the small device to me. I located the tuner and turned it slowly, listening for the signal to clear.

Garbled words and static suddenly clarified into an announcer's voice. "…day three of the manhunt."

"Yes, that," the ravens said in unison.

I shot them a surprised look. "A manhunt?"

The announcer continued.

"Stella Kormer escaped during a normal prisoner transport. She was supposed to be testifying for the state in the case against her husband regarding drug charges. The situation around her escape is still under investigation, though both guards insist she slipped her shackles and jumped out of the transport without assistance from anyone. There is some video evidence that supports this..."

I frowned at the twins, shooting the scowl at Rade, as well. "Okay, and?"

"Are you familiar with the powers of the Fourth Runespell?" she asked.

I ran the Runespells through my head. I didn't have them completely memorized, but I had an idea of each one. "Oh," I said.

"What is it?" Joseph asked me.

I turned to face him. "The Fourth Runespell can free the holder from anything that keeps them imprisoned."

He blinked and glanced down at the radio. "Oh!"

I turned back to Rade. "But why do you think this is about the Runespells? Is it just that her escape was weird?"

Rade pointed at the radio, and I lifted it up to listen again.

"...interviewing Kormer's cell-mate, Nancy Gaona, who was extradited from New Mexico only five months ago to face charges of fraud regarding her illegal medical practice and abetting her husband, Zaro Gaona, in multiple charges of abuse and tax evasion. The Gaona's began their organization in Vermont four years ago, giving Vermont jurisdictional priority. Zaro Gaona is being charged in absentia, as he is in a comatose state in Indiana University Health Methodist Hospital in Indiana..."

I choked on a gasp. My eyes stared but I couldn't focus on anything. The radio tumbled from my numb fingers. I felt Joseph wrap an arm around my shoulders. Voices spoke, but I couldn't understand what they said. I struggled with my breath as my head filled with a heavy feeling, and my consciousness fled.

CHAPT 5

I blinked my eyes and took a deep breath. I was sitting with my back to a large rock, the campfire crackling a few feet in front of me and the sunlight had faded from the sky. I looked around the camp and found Joseph sipping at a cup of something steaming. Rade and the twins sat at opposite sides of the fire.

I shifted, and Rade's eyes shot to my face.

"You're back," she said.

Joseph looked up at me. He set down his cup and filled up another. He put in a tea bag and brought it over to me.

"What happened?" he asked. "You moved and stuff, but you didn't speak or respond, like you weren't all there."

I blinked at him, taking in the concern on his face. "I-I'm not sure," I said. I glanced at Rade.

"It's the Berserker way," Rade offered. "The spirit warriors can't afford to faint in the middle of battle, so when something shocks them, they go into a fugue state instead. Functional, but not really conscious."

"How is that better?" Joseph asked.

Rade shrugged. "They can still move, walk, even carry things, and follow directions. In many situations, they won't be a hindrance to their compatriots. Not like if they just flopped over.

"Why would I do that?" I asked.

Joseph glanced at Rade. "Do you remember what they said on the radio? About the escapee?"

I screwed up my face, thinking. "Oh, yeah. Crap." I put my hands up over my cheeks. "Nancy was involved."

Rade nodded. "Do you understand why we think this woman has one of the Runespells?"

Nancy. Zaro's wife. Bob's accomplice. She'd been the one in charge of killing me in a "safe" manner and bringing me back after death. She'd been the one to remove my toes when they were damaged by the cold. She'd terrorized me during my recovery. And she'd wielded the Rod of Asclepius, healing people for money and saving the life of not so good ol' Bob.

I'd eventually read Nancy's confession statement about the Center. She and Zaro had set it up just to give them a place where she could work on healing Bob. She had focused on Bob and let Zaro do what he wanted with the Center's members. Like me. I couldn't believe their crazy agenda wouldn't corrupt virtually anyone they came in contact with, and their actions at the Center meant the Goana's had a lot of practice brainwashing people into doing their bidding. The idea that Nancy's cellmate escaped in a stroke of coincidence was too much to buy into.

I nodded. "So I guess our camping trip is over, huh?"

Joseph grimaced. "It was fun while it lasted."

Rade shook her head. "Actually, it seems this woman has fled along this very trail," she said. "If you turn around and go south on this path, you will have a good chance of finding her."

My eyebrows shot up. "A good chance? There's a lot of forest around here."

Rade nodded. "It will be important for you to use the other abilities the Berserker gives you. You will need to increase your training."

I rolled my eyes. "Of course. What abilities could I have that would help in this situation?"

Rade rolled her shoulders in a half shrug. "Mercy told me about what happened at your home. A full, untrained Berserker manifestation. She said you seemed to have a large cat spirit rather than a bear spirit, which is the most common." She stared into the fire for a moment. "Cat spirits tend to give agility, balance and tracking. And the ability to jump."

"Jump?" I said, unable to keep the skepticism from my voice. "I can already jump, you know."

Rade met my eyes. "I'm talking about jumping higher and farther than you probably should be able to."

I sighed and finished my tea. "So now I get to jump. Woo-hoo."

Joseph nudged me. "Don't knock it 'til you try it." He looked over at the Valkyrie and shape-shifted ravens. "In the meantime, I think we need a good night's sleep before we try to push anything else onto Nicola's plate."

•   •   •

I ran through a dark place, straining to get more speed. No matter how much I pushed myself, my muscles wouldn't do more than barely move. I struggled to force my body to move.

I could feel the thing behind me, dark and ominous. It had no real form, but the threat I felt from it drove me into a panic. I pushed harder and harder, nausea filling my gut when my efforts resulted in no real movement. I wanted to cry with frustration, but I didn't dare stop trying to run.

I slipped on some kind of slope in the darkness and fell, helpless into the black. I cried out, but my voice stuck in my throat. I could feel the thing getting closer, pressing in dangerously behind me. It threatened to engulf me, to swallow me whole.

I reached the bottom of the slope and scrambled on my hands and knees. The thing brushed my legs and the icy touch made me scream silently. I kicked out and tried to get to my feet. My limbs felt heavy and bogged down, like they'd gone numb.

One foot was engulfed by the thing, and I spun around to fight it. Instead, I fell on my back. Faces appeared in the darkness, the women and men from Zaro's cult, reaching out to hold me in place as the ice flowed over my body. I choked on my screams as the cold over-took me.

Joseph shook me awake, and I sat up with a small cry.

"You okay, Nicola?" he asked. "You kicked off your blankets in your sleep…"

I tried to speak, but my voice froze in my throat. He looked into my face and nodded. "It's about time to get up anyway," he said. "Let's get some hot tea."

•   •   •

"You need to find your trigger," Rade insisted, watching me go through the kata she'd shown me.

I panted with the effort. "I have plenty of triggers," I muttered.

"What angers you? What gives you the desire to be a righteous avenger? What makes you want to bring down the wrath of the gods?"

31

I paused and cocked my head to one side. Rade gave me an expectant look.

"What makes me want to bring down the wrath of the gods?" I kept my face straight when I met her eyes. "Bad movies and rap music."

Rade rolled her eyes. I'm pretty sure it wasn't something she did often. She was too uptight for that.

I went back to the series of moves. They were fighting moves, done in a set pattern and in slow motion. Katas, no matter what style of fighting was done, were about building muscle memory. The theory was, if I got in a fight, my body would remember the moves and play them out in double time.

I figured it was at least good exercise and it gave me something to focus on besides my continued failure to get past my past.

Rade moved up close to my side. She kept her voice low and stayed out of the way of my movements. But she spoke slowly, relentlessly. "What angers you? What causes your eyes to flash? What brings up the rage? What makes you want to hit, to hurt?"

I let her words wash over me as I moved. My mind only needed to partially focus on the kata. The rest of my thoughts drifted. A face appeared in my mind. Lupé. I'd gone to Zaro the first time to try to stop him from taking her as one of his many "wives." Instead, he'd taken me, and I'd never gotten a clear answer as to whether he'd left Lupé alone.

Thinking about how he'd manipulated so many, stealing their will for his own pleasure - stealing MY will for his pleasure - how he'd messed up so many people and families, how women abandoned their children for him... I could see the faces of the children at the Center, so many with a soul-deep sorrow spilling from their eyes.

I felt the anger bubbling up, and I let myself embrace it. There was no one I could hurt on accident here. Rade was more than capable of defending herself if I lost it, and Joseph was out of the way, making up some breakfast. The warmth rushed up the back of my neck, heating my ears and making my scalp tingle. Energy and power flowed up my legs and into my torso, spilling out along my arms.

My body felt like it had sprouted muscles. I glanced down at my hands and some manic part of my mind giggled over the thought that they should have turned green. I clenched my hands into fists and flexed my body. The tension pushed its way out of my gut, and I opened my mouth to roar my rage.

My vision changed, flooding red, then fading into a kind of yellow with blood red still tingeing the edges. I could still see everything, but I found that things were popping out at me, catching my attention in the odd yellow wash.

Rade was one of those things. She drew me like a flame attracts a moth. Her body and face sprang into sharp relief, and I could see in my mind which three spots to strike first for maximum pain.

I could also see on her face the exact moment when she understood that I would attack her. She shifted smoothly on her feet, changing the way her weight was distributed. Part of me knew she'd moved into a fighting stance, but the thoughts going through my head were hungry and challenging. The prey would be a good fight, and I could almost taste the pleasure of testing my strength on her.

I stepped towards her, my own feet moving step by step, a tiger stalking in the jungle. Prey could not run without exposing herself to my attack. I could take my time to get into position.

I hunched over slightly, coiling my body to be ready to spring, dropping my center of gravity to be more balanced. I let my mouth fall open, and I sniffed the air, letting my nose and tongue work together. I tasted the green of the trees and bushes, the yellow of sunlight warming the grass. A musky scent drifted past bringing to mind a deer scratching his cheek on a low branch.

I also smelled sweat. Not like human sweat, though it was impossible to explain the difference. Prey was nervous. I smiled. Then I lunged for the Valkyrie's throat.

CHAPT 6

The sweet sound of screams rang in my ears. I howled my anger and power, harmonizing with the high-pitched shrieks. Rough hands pulled me back and the sane part of my mind latched on to the familiar, deep voice yelling my name.

I shook my head and let the colors drained from my vision. Strength drained from my limbs, and I lay back, panting, and tried to get my bearings.

Joseph stood over me, his hands up as if to block me. He shot a glance over his shoulder, and I caught the worried expression on his face. I followed his gaze to Rade. She had several red lumps on her face that would bruise up later. A few cuts accentuated the injuries. She was bent over someone lying on the ground, and three others stood over her.

I frowned. "Too many people," I muttered. My tongue felt too big for my mouth, and I heard a slight slur in my words.

Joseph shot me a look. "Yeah," he said. "We have guests."

I shook my head out and struggled to my feet. Joseph didn't offer to help. Two guys, dressed in typical hiking gear for the season, flinched back from me. The third person standing, a woman, glared at me.

Rade looked up from the person lying on the ground. "Your friend will be fine," she said to the three hikers. "She took a solid punch to the jaw, but no real damage."

"Real damage?" the other woman snapped. "You people should be arrested! You can't just attack someone like that!"

I frowned and looked at Joseph. "Did I attack them?" I asked quietly.

He made a face and gestured for me to wait, his attention on the newcomers and Rade.

The Valkyrie stood up, helping the injured woman to her feet. The woman worked her jaw tenderly but seemed okay.

Rade glared at the woman who had spoken. "While your friend had her heart in the right place, she interrupted a sparring session without the slightest clue as to what was going on," Rade said. "Her injury was unfortunate, but it was, frankly, the result of your own actions."

"She was trying to help you!" the woman yelled, stepping forward to get in Rade's face. "That crazy bitch was beating the crap out of you!"

Rade lifted an eyebrow, her cold eyes impassive. "I did not ask for help," she said. "I assure you, I am capable of handling the 'crazy bitch.' In fact, I yelled for you to stay away."

The woman lifted a finger, pointing it into the Valkyrie's face. "You people are fucking nuts, and I will be reporting this to the police!"

Rade glanced down at the finger and back at the woman. The hikers hesitated, then went a shade pale before every one of them took a step back. "Do what you must," Rade said. "However, keep in mind that you should not step between two fighters sparring again before you know what the situation is."

The Valkyrie turned her back on the hikers and walked towards me. I backed away a step, and she hesitated, offering me a quick smile. For her, that was practically the same as grinning.

I glanced behind her as the hikers gathered up their comrade and made their way back onto the main trail. "That was—"

"Unnecessary," Joseph interjected. "The two of you are going to get us arrested."

I shrugged my shoulders uncomfortably. "I didn't mean to—"

"You did fine," Rade cut in. She shot a glance at Joseph. "It is difficult for those outside the situation to understand what is going on."

Joseph snorted. "Nicola was going to town on your face, that's what was going on." He turned back to me. "Why would you do that to someone, Nicola? It's not like you to just keep hurting people like that."

I gaped at him. "I-I—"

Rade watched him closely. "You don't understand either," she said, quietly.

"What's to understand?" Joseph turned on the Valkyrie. His voice rose with his anger. "You are supposed to be helping us, helping her, and she was beating you! With her fists!"

Joseph's voice cracked to a high pitch, and I suddenly realized that he was scared. Of me.

I put my hand on his arm and spoke quietly. "Joseph, please. I need to hear what Rade has to say about this so I can understand what I was doing." I glanced at her. "I was able to control when it started, wasn't I?"

The blonde woman nodded. "Yes. Finally." She shifted on her feet. "You found something that let you embrace the Berserker."

Joseph growled, "If that's the Berserker you've been so hot to bring out, I think maybe it was just fine where it was."

I leveled a look at my friend. "Leaving it as it was would be suppression, Joseph. Wouldn't that be just as bad?"

He flushed and looked embarrassed. "Well, yeah, but…"

Rade cut in. "The Berserker will return, eventually," she warned. "It is better to have control over it, practice with it, rather than have it come out and hurt anything in its path until it, and Nicola, burns out."

"You aren't concerned about your face?" Joseph snapped at her.

Rade shrugged. "I am created to fight," she said. "I can take the blows, and the damage will heal quickly. It is better that the Berserker attack me than you, don't you think?"

Joseph went pale and shot a look at me. I cocked an eyebrow at him, shooting him a look that suggested he was an idiot for thinking I would hurt him. I waited for the concern on his face to relax before I grinned. "You wouldn't like me when I'm angry," I intoned.

He snorted. "Whatever," he said, rolling his eyes. He focused on Rade. "We have to get going if we are going to make it to town tomorrow. We are almost out of supplies."

I perked up. "A real bed?"

Joseph grimaced and patted my head. "We'll see. We have to get there first."

Rade glanced at the sun. "Very well," she said. "But I want to meet again before you leave the trail."

Joseph started to protest, but Rade cut him off. "This is a delicate time in Nicola's progress," she pointed out. "Leaving it with what just happened could cause more harm than good."

Joseph nodded. "Fine," he grumbled, shrugging into his pack. "See you tonight then?"

•   •   •

"You did it before," Rade pointed out. "Just do it again."

I shifted my shoulders. "I tried that," I said. "I can't help that the emotional push isn't there this time."

The Valkyrie frowned. "Well, what do you feel?" she asked.

I scowled. "Frustration, annoyance," I said. I caught her look and rolled my eyes. "I'm afraid I won't be able to bring out the Berserker again. I'm afraid of what going Berserk will mean for me. I feel doubt about my part in this whole thing." I flung an arm wide, gesturing.

Joseph sat up straighter. He'd insisted on watching, promising to stay out of the way when we sparred. "You could quit," he said.

Rade and I turned to stare at him.

He shrugged. "You don't seem happy with this," he said. "So pass the torch. Let someone more willing to take up the whole hero, quest thing."

I frowned. Had I told Joseph how my stint as a hero would end? I couldn't remember, but surely I hadn't, or he wouldn't be suggesting such a thing.

Joseph looked from me to Rade and back again. "What?" he asked. "Don't you know how to turn in your two weeks?" He looked at Rade. "What's the procedure for that?"

Rade shot me a confused glance, and I sighed. "Joseph," I said. "There is only one way to pass the torch, as you said." I hesitated, unsure how to say it. "This is a lifetime gig," I offered.

He scowled. "Lifetime? What—" Comprehension dawned on his face.

Rade nodded. "She must complete the quest or die. That is how it ends."

Joseph's face went pale as he turned to me. "That's crazy!" he said. "I mean, who signs up for this kind of thing?"

I shrugged. "You were there, remember?" I pointed out. "I guess there should have been more focus on the fine print."

"How did you find out about this... fine print?"

"The hospital," I said. "After the fire. Odin and Mercy came to talk."

Rade snorted. "I heard about that," she said. "You threatened to refuse the quest, even knowing the penalty."

Joseph whistled. "Seriously?"

I shrugged one shoulder. "I had to," I said. "If I let them push me into it without pushing back, I would have gotten pissy and bitter at them for all this crap happening. I had to take it on my own terms."

Joseph shook his head. "Are you telling me you threatened to choose death just to make a point?"

I pursed my lips. "Yeah, pretty much." I smiled at him. "I gotta do things my way, you know that."

He nodded. "I just..." He looked at me, a serious expression on his face. "You've been carrying this quest-or-death thing around for years, by yourself?"

I shrugged.

Joseph shook his head. "Damn, no wonder you are all emotionally constipated."

"Hey!"

"We gotta have some deep dark conversations, Nicola," he said. "When's the last time you did a dark soul meditation?"

I thought back to the experience I had with a monster in the dark at the Healing Center last year. "I dealt with what Zaro did, Joseph. I had to, in order to face him down."

He rolled his eyes. "And since?"

I shrugged.

"You know better than that," he said. "It's an ongoing process."

"We really don't have time—" Rade began.

Joseph cut her off, slashing his hand through the air. "You don't have time not to," he said. "You are getting nowhere right now."

I nodded. "Fine. What do you suggest?"

CHAPT 7

"I don't know about this," I said to Joseph, sitting up.

He pressed his hand against my shoulder, pushing me back to lay on my bedroll. "Look, I know you said you'd gotten addicted to the astral last year, but you haven't been going in much since, have you?"

"No," I admitted, shifting on the bedroll. "But I also haven't been in a situation like this since then."

Joseph watched me closely. "You know what the dangers are, Nicola." He took a deep breath. "I think you need to find out what your spirit guides have to say about this."

I stared up at him for a long moment, then nodded. "Okay," I said. "Let's do this."

Joseph moved to his own bedroll, laying back and shifting around a bit. I closed my eyes and pulled up memories of the spirit world. My mind brought out the random things I'd experienced recently.

I perceived the energies and souls around me most of the time but pushed the sights and sounds away from my consciousness so they wouldn't distract me from interacting with the so-called real world. It wouldn't do for me to jump at every wolf and hawk that roamed along the Appalachian Trail. I'd end up falling off a steep slope or twisting my ankle.

I recalled the dark horse spirit that had pranced alongside one of the hikers we'd passed. Most people had a spirit or two around them, often mammals, though I'd seen my share of lizards and snakes, birds of prey, and even a shark once, gliding silently in the air beside a bouncer outside a bar. Less obvious were the other spirit guides, like an oak tree that grew up behind a family matriarch as she herded her family through a superstore, or lava flowing around a teenager wearing black clothes and an impassive expression.

I let the subtle feeling of the spirit world fill me, taking my consciousness through the veil. I found myself floating up away from the planet, past the moon. I dove into the deep blackness between the stars, swimming on eddies of solar waves. I let myself play for a moment, partially because I needed the relaxation but also because I was putting off the next step. After a moment, I sighed and stepped into the astral plane.

I didn't need to go through the entire process, not since I'd had so much practice the previous year, but there was a certain satisfaction in going through the preparations again. I opened my mind's eye to the astral world. The surrealism of it was a familiar sight. Trees dripped leaves, literally like water droplets, nearby, and a family of what looked like pteradons flew past me, upside down. The silver-blue of the Bifrost cut across the sky, never more than a few dozen yards away.

I turned and spotted a school of air swimmers, mermaids who traveled through the sky instead of water. Their fins were huge and silky, like beta fish fins, but they had the torsos and faces of women. In general, they were mischievous but not dangerous, but the blood drained from my face when I saw them.

I gasped as the memories came flooding over me: icy numbness, fear, hopelessness. I'd seen air swimmers when I'd fled to the astral during my death at the hands of Nancy and the Healing Center. I struggled with the emotions roiling within me, trying to get them under control. If I let them go too long, the astral would reflect those feelings.

A dark blob of something that looked like tar or mud appeared at my side. It opened a huge maw of sharp teeth and snapped it down on my arm. I threw back my head and howled in pain and fear, wresting my limb from its grasp. It released me with a juicy sucking pop, and I stumbled back a few steps into something squishy. I turned to find another of the creatures ready to engulf my upper body. I screeched and dove away from the Fear.

Others appeared, some the black dripping blobs, others, like wispy shadows flowing over me. One shadow wrapped itself around my throat while a smaller blob clamped down on my calf. I opened my mouth to scream again, and another shadow slipped into my mouth, filling my head until I thought my skull would burst from the pressure.

Tears leaked from my eyes as I fell to my hands and knees. There were too many of them and terror filled my mind. All I could think of was getting away from the creatures. I lashed out with hands and legs, dislodging them more by luck than skill. I crawled away from them on my hands and knees, but they followed, making a game of snapping at my feet.

I spotted a cliff in front of me, and I launched myself to my feet. If I could get over it, I would be able to get free of them long enough to regain control of my astral experience. I lifted one foot to leap over the cliff and crashed to the ground. One of the blobs had wrapped an appendage around my other foot. I clawed at the ground as they swarmed over me, screams tearing at my throat.

"Nicola!"

Joseph's voice cut through the breathy laughing and smacking pops from the Fears. I wrenched my head around and spotted him rushing towards me. He was wearing shiny knight's armor and carrying what looked like a hockey stick made of glowing silver.

He swung the stick across the line of Fears between us, flinging the creatures away. He pushed closer to me and yelled in my face. "Step out of the astral, Nicola! Now!"

I blinked at him and the realization washed over me. I just had to leave the astral. I didn't have to escape the creatures first. My own fear of them kept me trapped here, not them.

I nodded at Joseph and slipped back into my body. I sat up on the bedroll, my breath catching in my throat. Reflexively, I checked my body for injuries. There were no scratches or bite marks, but I could still feel the soreness of the spiritual wounds.

After a moment, Joseph sat up, much more slowly and calmly than I had. He looked over at me.

I held up my hands. "I know, I know," I muttered. "Rookie mistakes."

He shook his head. "It's worse than I thought," he said. "And I get it; you tried to tell me."

I grimaced at him, and he sighed, staring at me as if I could give him the answers he was looking for.

"Let's get some sleep," he said, finally. "We've got a lot of work to do."

•   •   •

Joseph led me down a steep slope out of the trees. I blinked at the shock of seeing a bustling city that carried on just out of sight of where we had been on the trail a few moments ago. We lengthened our strides as the rocks and brush gave way to grass, and the dirt trail turned into gravel, then cement as we made our way into the edges of the town.

Joseph knew where he was going, so I kept my head down and concentrated on my breathing. The sounds of cars and just urban noise grated on my senses. Even at home, I was usually in a more rural and natural setting.

We came to a stop at a coffee shop, and Joseph held the door for me. I sent him a questioning look but held my tongue while we ordered some turkey on bagel sandwiches and sugary espresso filled drinks.

We sat with our order, letting the heavy packs slide off our shoulders. Joseph pulled out his phone and tapped at the screen.

"Okay," I said. "I'm not arguing the stop for good coffee, but I thought we had supplies to pick up."

Joseph nodded, barely glancing up from his phone. "Yup." He tapped a few more times. "How does blueberry yogurt sound?"

I scowled. "Delicious," I said. "But—"

He held up his phone and I let the scowl slide off my face. "Online ordering," he explained. "We sip coffee until it's ready to pick up."

I sat back and heaved a sigh. "I love technology!"

Joseph smiled as he continued tapping. I stared out the window and slurped my creamy caramel java.

"There!" he said, dropping the phone on the table. "Supplies ordered. Motel reserved. Coffee in hand. Hot showers tonight."

I threw my head back and laughed. "Oooh, baby!" I purred. "Talk dirty to me some more!"

We ate and sipped at the coffee until a text message popped up telling us that the order was ready. Since the store we were picking up from was just a few blocks away, and across the street from the motel, we made short work of grabbing the bags and getting our errands run before checking in.

After taking showers and completely unpacking, sorting and repacking our backpacks, we ordered Chinese food and lounged on the beds until the food came.

"I was worried about you, you know." Joseph picked at his lo mien with his chopsticks.

I dipped my crab rangoon in the unnaturally red sauce and ate half of it in one bite. "Yeah, I get that," I said. "But it's not something you have experience with." I paused, chewing as I thought about how to explain the situation. "I just don't know how you could understand all the complexities. It's like being in a job with things like 'industry standards' and jargon. There's a lot of stuff in the background to understand."

Joseph sent me a scowl. "I get that you have this gift—"

I snorted at the word.

"But," he continued. "I can see what you're doing, and I'm not sure you are aware of the direction you might be heading in."

I sat back pushing the scraps of my almond chicken away from me. "And what direction do you think I'm going in?"

"You barely noticed when you were pummeling Rade," he said. "And you didn't skip a beat when that woman tried to break you up." He leaned forward, and I could read the earnest expression on his face. "You literally turned and punched her without hesitation, Nicola."

I grimaced. "Damn," I mumbled. I stared at the garish pattern on the bedspread for a moment before I shook my head to clear it. "It makes sense, though. If I'm in a fight like that, I can't afford to evaluate every situation and person."

Joseph's eyebrows went up.

I held up my hands. "I have a job to do, and I might have to stop people quickly and violently, and other people could come in and try to do the 'right thing' by stopping me."

"You think that's right?" Joseph asked.

I pursed my lips. "It's like this," I said. "If you come across a woman cowering while a man is whaling on another man, can you tell me what happened? Is it a mugger trying to take out the woman's date? Is it a guy who is beating up a rapist he caught in the act?" I met Joseph's gaze. "In that situation, if the bad guy gets away, at least you stopped him, right?"

Joseph nodded. "Not ideal, but at least you wouldn't be hurting an innocent."

I shook my head. "If the bad guy is a serial rapist? A serial killer?" I grabbed the fortune cookie and snapped it open. "What if the guy you have to stop only needs a brief window to destroy everything? Like a bomber with the trigger in his hand? Can you afford to let someone stop you until you can explain the situation to them? Can you take that chance?" I shook my head. "When that much is on the line, taking everyone out and sorting it all later becomes a very real option."

Joseph considered my words while I chomped on my cookie. I glanced at the fortune in my hand. *The truth will reveal itself in surprising ways.* I pressed my lips together. That didn't sound as hopeful as it might have only a few years ago.

Joseph shook his head. "I just think it's going to end badly," he said. "The first time you hurt someone that didn't deserve it, you are going to hate yourself for that. And people are going to see you as the kind of person who hurts others."

I snorted. "Like who?" I snapped. His words dug into me, making me feel angry and upset. "Who is going to see me like that, who I would even care about seeing me like that? Why should I be worried about random people's feelings about me?"

Joseph dropped his head, playing with the sauce left from his meal. "Like me," he murmured.

My eyes opened wide, and I could feel my eyebrows crawling up into my hairline. "You would?" I whispered. "You would think that I would hurt someone intentionally? Without a damn good reason?"

Joseph's head snapped up. "I think you would get so involved in your damn issues and your stupid quest that you would forget that other people are... are just as deserving of your focus as those stupid pendants!"

I swung my legs over and slid off the bed. "Screw you!" I grabbed my jacket and checked the pocket for my ID and emergency money. As my hand touched the door handle, I hesitated, glancing back at him.

He sat there, impassive, with a hurt look in his eyes. "I think I might have been wrong before," he said. "I think maybe your priorities aren't as solid as I'd thought. You're messed up, Nicola. I'm sorry I have to tell you this."

"Don't be," I snapped and slammed out of the room.

Chapt 8

The sun was starting to set, but it was still bright outside. I stalked along the sidewalk ignoring the people I passed and not paying attention to the direction I was going. After a few blocks, my frustration faded enough for me to focus on a destination. It took me only a moment to locate a hole-in-the-wall bar.

I wasn't a big drinker, but the anonymity and ambiance of being a faceless, random drinker in a dive bar appealed to me. I opened the door and my face relaxed when I saw how few patrons there were. This was not a place where people came to socialize. This was a place for drowning sorrows. Perfect.

I flopped down in a chair in a dark corner and asked for a whiskey and coke when the waitress, a middle-aged woman, shuffled up. The TV was on, and I had a good view of it. The end of a football game caught my attention, as grown men slammed into each other, desperate to break the tie their teams were locked into.

My drink arrived, and I sipped at it, alternating staring at the TV and getting lost in my thoughts as I replayed the fight with Joseph over and over. When the first drink was emptied, I glanced around and found the waitress watching her customers. I motioned for another drink and she nodded.

I took a moment to check out the rest of the patrons in the bar. A few older men slouched on bar stools over beers and shots. Another table held a couple of guys dressed in the dusty-dirty clothes and huge boots of construction workers. They talked quietly while drinking from brown bottles and pointing to the game on the screen.

A few other people, men and woman sat or mingled, but it was pretty quiet except for the strains of music that mixed pop-country and 90s alt-rock. The bartender shuffled from one end of the bar to the other, mixing drinks, cleaning and taking payments without stopping for more than a second. He was obviously not the type to double as a therapist for his patrons.

I slouched back in my chair, letting my head fall back. Heat filled my temples and warmed my cheeks as the alcohol moved into my system. I was a total lightweight and I knew it, but the feeling soothed my frayed nerves. I relaxed, knowing I wouldn't have to be on guard too much in this place. Even the guys barely shot me a look, not looking for a hook-up.

The news came on and I watched, curious about what exciting events could have gone on while I was trekking through the woods. After some story about an embarrassing incident between the President and some foreign dignitary, the talking heads brought up the manhunt.

I sat up, eager for some news that could point me in the right direction. Heck, maybe the authorities would catch this Stella, and I could just pay her a visit, get the Runespell and go home.

"...Search for Stella Kormer may continue through the end of the week. She is not believed to be armed, but police are warning people to avoid confronting Kormer, if possible. She is thought to be in the Norwich-Hanover area. If anyone sees Kormer, you can call..."

I stared at the screen, the picture of a haggard-looking woman with purple circles under her eyes and shoulder-length, dirty-blonde hair staring back at me. She didn't look like a religious fanatic or someone looking for power. She looked sad, beaten.

I slammed back the remainder of my drink and dropped some bills on the table. I had a job to do and, like it or not, I needed Joseph's help to safely navigate the trail. I could swallow being hurt by his words if he stepped up to get this done. The rest we'd work out later. Or not.

"Hey, bitch!"

My head whipped around at the man's voice. I spotted a man at the bar with his hand locked around the wrist of a woman with short hair. Part of my mind noticed that the cut was really bad, choppy and bedraggled. The rest of me focused on the man.

"What is your problem, buddy?" I shouted, stalking up to him. "Let her go!"

The man started to protest, and I grabbed his wrist, applying pressure on the bones until he yelped and his hand opened. I shoved his hand away and stuck my finger in his face.

"What the fuck do you think you're doing?" I demanded.

The man scowled at me. "What do you think *you're* doing? That woman was just on the news."

I blinked, backing off. "What?"

The man hefted himself of his bar stool. "You heard me," he said. "She's that chick all the cops are looking for. And you let her get away."

I turned around, but the woman was already gone. I heard the man yell after me, but I hit the door at a run. I stopped when I hit the sidewalk, my eyes darting around for any sign of the woman. Night had fallen, and the streetlights gave uneven illumination for a search. A running figure caught my attention and I rushed after her.

She was almost two blocks ahead of me, but I let my stride lengthen and I found my pace. Since the events in Indianapolis a few years ago, I'd half-heartedly tried to get into better shape. I began gaining ground on the woman, keeping my eyes locked on her olive green jacket, just before she headed for the sidewalk that led back to the trail. I pushed my muscles harder, determined to catch her before she reached the cover of the dark woods.

The number of people on the sidewalk faded away before my feet hit the gravel path with a steady crunch-crunch. I saw the woman stop and duck down ahead of me. She pulled a backpack out from behind a bush next to the path and glanced back at me. She took off running again, but I'd gained several yards and was right behind her when the trail sloped up. We slowed down to make it up the incline, and I was hit by a sudden wave of nausea.

The alcohol in my system had finally overcome the adrenaline rush I'd been running on. A sudden wave of vertigo caused me to stumble sideways a few steps. I struggled to recover and pushed my muscles to climb the trail. The woman reached the trees a few moments before I did. I struggled with the urge to vomit and pushed onto the main trail. My breath heaved raggedly and my face burned with exertion combined with an alcohol flush. I glanced up the trail each way but found no sign of her. I took a deep breath, fighting another wave of dizziness.

A branch snapped and I took off in that direction. I rounded a bend in the trail and spotted the green jacket and gray backpack ahead of me. I put on a burst of speed and caught up to her, slamming into her back. The woman fell forward to her hands and knees with a cry. She scrambled up and I set my feet in the stance for the first move of the kata I'd been practicing. Her face was weary and she watched me with a cautious expression.

"What do you want?" she asked.

My eyes narrowed. "You are Stella Kormer."

The woman sighed. "Trying to be a hero, huh? Gonna catch me and take me back?"

I lifted my jaw. "Sure. Why not?"

She shrugged. "Yeah," she said. "Why not?" Moonlight filtered through the leaves swaying in the wind. A stray beam lit her face for a moment, and I was struck by how defeated she appeared.

I relaxed my stance. "Just come with me, Stella," I said. "You don't have to do this."

Her lips pressed together. "I didn't do what they said," she said. "It was Johnny did it, but they put it on both of us."

I nodded. Nausea and dizziness had crept back in, and I blinked my eyes rapidly to keep my focus. "Sounds like a shit situation," I said.

"No one deserves to be imprisoned by the people they loved," she said. "No one deserves to be punished for being conned."

I nodded again, struggling to understand her words as my supper and drinks tried to make a break from my stomach. I didn't even see her move. Lights exploded behind my eyes and I was on my stomach on the dirt path before I knew it. I struggled to get to my hands and knees as Stella disappeared around the next bend.

I shifted to get to my feet, and my stomach finally won the battle. I heaved into the bushes for several minutes before I could stop the retching. I rocked back, sitting on my heels with my arms braced in front of me for several minutes, panting. Finally, the chill night air seeped into my bones and my consciousness. A jolt of fear gave me enough strength to get to my feet and stagger my way back to the hotel.

CHAPT 9

Joseph took one look at me and insisted I wait until morning. He ignored all of my protests, pointing out that it was almost suicidal to run through the woods in the middle of the night. I nearly won the argument until he pulled out his ace.

"It'll be too cold, Nicola," he said. "You'd be risking hypothermia."

I heaved a sigh and crawled into bed, thankful that Joseph wasn't going to bring up our previous conversation just yet. I tossed and turned all night and was up at dawn, ready to go.

Joseph pointed out that we wouldn't get much distance on the escapee if we didn't eat first, so we stopped at a chain restaurant that specialized in pancakes and waffles.

The hostess took one look at us and broke into a smile. "You must be Joseph and Nicola? Your friend insisted on the party room for your table. I understand mid-vacation business meetings can be stressful, so I'll have your server get your order immediately so you can have some privacy."

Joseph and I exchanged a glance, but the young woman kept up a running monologue, preventing us from correcting her obvious mistake.

"Here you go!" she bubbled. She turned to the man at the corner table in the private party room. "Mr. Tyr, your friends have arrived."

I looked at the man I'd met only once before, about a year before. He stood, holding one arm close to his body. He waved to the other chairs with the other hand.

"What's going on?" I asked. I caught Joseph's frown. "Oh, you two haven't met. Joseph, this is Tyr. Tyr, Joseph."

Joseph blinked and nodded. "Yeah, I saw you at the bar..."

Tyr bobbed his head in greeting. "So you did."

We sat and the server came in for our orders. We waited until she brought the drinks before I asked again, "What are you doing here?"

Tyr frowned. "It is a grave situation, what you are facing."

I shrugged. "Just an escaped convict," I said. "Just because she got away last night—"

The one-handed god leaned forward. "You almost had her?"

I hung my head. "Yeah, keyword: almost."

Tyr shook his head. "It would have been better had you caught her, but it is what it is. Unfortunately, it means the news I have is still vital."

We paused as the server brought our food in. My stomach churned at the smell of bacon and syrup, but I sipped at my juice to calm it. I knew from experience that my system would settle down once it got a little food, so I started in on my fruit bowl. Joseph poured a ton of syrup on his Belgian waffle and dipped his sausages into it before taking a bite.

Tyr waited until the server stepped out of the room and closed the door before leaning towards us. "There is a reason that this woman has chosen the Appalachian Trail as her escape route," he said.

"She likes nature?" I asked hopefully.

The god shook his head. "Once upon a time, I made a judgment call that cost me dearly."

I nodded, but Joseph's face showed confusion.

"We knew that the wolf would one day be a part of a series of events that would lead to Ragnarok," Tyr explained. "His nature would be that of destruction and death."

"Would be?" Joseph asked.

Tyr nodded. "Until that point, he did not display signs of such behavior. In fact, he was raised by the Æsir until his size created some concerns." The god sighed. "We had the dwarves create the chain, Gleipnir, and we asked him to let us bind him, as we had already tried before."

I dug into my pancakes. "He didn't trust you to release him if the chains held."

The god nodded. "He trusted me most of all. So I placed my hand into his mouth as a sign of faith that we would release him."

Joseph scowled. "You lied."

"Yes," Tyr said. "I lied." He held up his remaining hand when Joseph opened his mouth again. "And we had considered that our actions would create the bloodlust we feared in him. We are not fools, mortal."

"So why would you do that?" Joseph demanded. "Why not just leave him be? He was innocent when you chained him."

Tyr nodded. "Yes, he was." He held up his mangled wrist. "I see this as a just penalty for my part in that."

Joseph dropped his fork onto his empty plate and sat back, crossing his arms over his chest. "That doesn't explain why."

"We had a lot of information to work with, but we didn't know what would be the cause of some things," Tyr said. "We knew he would become a monster, eventually." He leveled his gaze at Joseph. "In the end, it came down to a simple fact: we couldn't take the chance. The risk was too great, and the stakes were too high."

Joseph snorted. "Seems stupid to me," he said, nodding at the god's missing hand. "You certainly didn't come out of it very well."

Tyr tilted his head to one side. "How do you think I should come out of that?" he asked. "How do you think Nicola should come out of this?"

Joseph frowned. "I-I don't know," he said. "I guess, you know, she's the hero. She should come out of it... well, heroically?"

The god nodded. "And what does that look like?"

Joseph leaned forward, bracing his elbows on the table and pursing his lips thoughtfully. "Heroes are the good guys. They have honor and integrity. They are honest and noble, and they do the right thing."

Tyr gave us a sad smile. "That's very nice," he said. "All tidy and happily ever after. Who in the Nine Worlds gave you the impression that that's how life works?"

Joseph gaped. "Well... I, I guess... I don't know."

"Hollywood," I suggested. "Fiction from the romantic period."

Tyr nodded and leaned forward, staring into Joseph's face. "Heroes go to war, one way or another," he said, his voice low and calm, but as hard as iron. "Heroes fight and die. And the dead ones—"

"Go to Valhalla," Joseph cut in. "I know that part."

"But did you know that it's not the ideal afterlife?" Tyr asked. "Did you know that fighting in Ragnarok is a kind of consolation prize for those who cannot join their families in the afterlife?"

Joseph frowned. "But you guys are all about the fighting..."

I shook my head but kept silent as Tyr continued.

"We are all about family," he corrected Joseph in a quiet voice. "The fighting is a necessity. The fighting is how we keep the Jötun from sweeping over the world. The fighting is our sacrifice for you mortals." He sat back. "And for our sacrifice, we've watched you turn the harsh and horrible reality of war and battle and fighting into a grand, idealized thing to praise."

Joseph glanced at me, and I nodded. "It's true," I said. "Family first. Kith and kin. Blood and ancestors, clan and lands. That's what Heathens are supposed to be about." I sipped my juice. "And the blood part is metaphorical, not some genetic purity bullshit."

"What's that got to do with Nicola?" Joseph asked.

"Sacrifice," Tyr said. "Realistically, heroes don't come out of it okay."

"You mean, they are likely to die," Joseph said.

"No," Tyr shook his head. "It's possible, of course, but even the heroes who don't die won't come out of it okay. To become a hero is to sacrifice yourself."

Joseph looked at me. "What is he talking about?"

I sucked on my teeth for a moment. "You know how you said you were worried about me doing stuff I would regret? Stuff I might not be able to live with?"

He nodded. "Yeah."

I shrugged my shoulders. "That's not something I'm worried will happen. It's something I'm certain will happen."

He turned back to Tyr. "Are you serious?"

The god nodded solemnly. "The sacrifice is of who we are, not just of our lives. We do what needs to be done, even when it's hard, even when it's not black and white, even when we aren't really sure it's the right choice."

"And because we need to be able to do that to stop the enemy," I broke in, "to fight the fight, we have to come to terms with the fact that we aren't making it out intact. We have to be willing to come back from war broken or not at all, or we are useless in the fight."

Tyr held up his stump, flaps of skin hanging in ragged edges. "I am the god of justice, the god of honor and integrity. I am the god of honesty and truth."

He looked at the stump, sorrow written on his features. "I undermined all of that to do what needed to be done. Because I have been all of those things,

I was the only one who could lie to the wolf." He shook his head and let his arm fall back against his stomach. "I still don't know that it was the right thing to do, but it was the best I could do at the time. And that's all a hero can do."

I stirred the remaining drips of syrup around on my plate. "We'll never get out of this alive!"

Joseph rounded on me. "You are cracking jokes about this? You are talking about possibly putting your very soul in jeopardy, of undermining everything you've ever stood for."

"Yeah," I said. "We are."

"And you're okay with that?" he demanded.

"Okay?" I shook my head. "No, not at all. But it's what I agreed to, and anything less results in a nunya situation."

"Nunya?"

I smirked. "As in, nunya gonna survive that shit. You do remember Ragnarok, right?" I waved my hands around. "All the various apocalypses playing out in full Technicolor? End of the world?" I gestured at his empty plate. "No more waffles?"

Joseph rolled his eyes at me. "Well, yeah, but—"

"Why would you think," Tyr asked in an even voice, "that stopping something so big, so major would not exact a price that would make most people run the other way?"

I snorted. "Don't kid yourself. I still want to run the other way." I pressed my lips together and choked back a sob. "But I can't let Ella, and Maria - I can't just let them die because it's hard to do the thing. I can't let everyone suffer because my ego includes standing by my convictions to the detriment of the whole damn world."

Joseph sat back in his chair. "I just don't see why you can't do both. Save the world and keep your morals intact."

I shrugged. "I can try, but when is the last time battles worth fighting were fair?"

CHAPT 10

"So what does this all have to do with why Stella Kormer is on the Appalachian Trail?" I asked. I avoided Joseph's gaze. He was just too invested in keeping me the way I'd always been, and that would get everyone killed.

Tyr sighed. "We put the wolf in a place far away from the Norse people," he said. "It wasn't an unpopulated area, but those who lived nearby were inclined to leave things that were out of the ordinary be."

I dropped my head into my hands and groaned. When I lifted my face, I let my hands drag over my cheeks. "Say it ain't so," I pleaded. "Tell me Fenrir, the monstrous wolf, son of Loki, destined killer of the Allfather himself, isn't trapped somewhere along the Trail."

Tyr grimaced. "I'm sorry," he said. "Ms. Kormer is heading in that direction."

Joseph frowned. "So what? You said it yourself: those chains are unbreakable."

Tyr nodded.

"All magic has a loophole," I pointed out. "And Stella has the Runespell of getting out of anything that imprisons."

Joseph's eyebrows rose to impossible heights on his brow. "Could she really set him free?"

Tyr shrugged. "It's never been tested," he said. "But if anything could free him before his time, that pendant would be it."

●　　　●　　　●

I followed Joseph along the path back to the main trail. We turned the direction Stella had taken, and I carefully avoiding looking at the spot where I'd thrown up after getting my ass handed to me.

Joseph dropped back to walk beside me and noticed my reaction. "So what happened last night?"

I sighed. "I had a few drinks and got in over my head," I muttered. "She was ready for anything, and I was... I was being nice."

"Nice?" he said. "How so?"

I shrugged. "Some guy in the bar grabbed this woman, and I jumped in to save her," I said. "I pried his hand off her before he could explain why he'd grabbed her. She had just been on the news - great big picture and everything - and I completely missed it all."

Joseph shrugged. "It happens," he said. He was trying to reassure me, I knew, but it wasn't what I needed him to understand.

"No, Joseph," I snapped. "You just don't get it. I let her go. I pulled my punches. And now, the one person I needed to catch slipped away." I snorted. "I helped her get away from me. How crap-tastic is that?"

Joseph frowned, stopping to face me. "You were just trying to do what's right," he said, reaching out to touch my arm.

"That's the point!" I cried, jerking away from him. "I can't afford to do what's right. I need to do what's necessary."

He frowned at me, and I saw the hurt in his eyes. I felt sorry for him. Black and white was so much easier to grasp, and even when you knew that the world didn't work like that, it was hard to deal with it when the shades of gray slapped you in the face. But I couldn't hold his hand while he worked through those emotions. I didn't have time to deal with his issues with what I had to do. I had to find a way to drive the point home or drive him away.

I shook my head in wonder. "Have you completely missed what Tyr said? What Rade said? We've been trying to tell you. I don't get the luxury of being some white knight, holier-than-thou paladin." I pushed past him. "I'm too busy saving the world," I snarled over my shoulder.

I stalked down the trail, my ears straining for signs of what my friend was doing behind me. After a long moment, I heard his footsteps on the trail. I released a breath I hadn't realized I'd been holding when I realized he was following me.

I blinked away tears. Maybe I wasn't going to be left alone in this after all.

•   •   •

I crouched on the ground, shielding my abdomen from attack. Joseph stepped out of the trees and I glanced up at him. He stopped in his tracks, looking from me to the Valkyrie standing over me.

"Uh, what's up, chicas?" he said, forcing a brightness into his voice.

I rolled my eyes and let Rade give me a hand up. My stomach roiled from the blow she'd given me only a moment ago. "You know what's up, Joseph," I said. "Rade is kicking my ass, just like every other day for the last week."

Joseph frowned. "Still not vamping out?"

I shook my head.

Rade scowled. "Vampires are nothing to joke about," she said.

Joseph and I stared at her for a moment.

Her face relaxed just a little. "I'm kidding," she offered. We relaxed, then she added, "Vampires are relatively easy to defeat if you know what you're doing."

"Sweet baby Baldur, Rade!" I cried. "That's not helpful. At all."

She shrugged. "The truth is always helpful, in its own way and in its own time."

I stumbled over to Joseph. "I think I'm done with Norse Yoda for now," I said. "What did you find out?"

Joseph eyed Rade cautiously for a moment. He'd gone to talk to some fellow hikers who had camped near us the previous night.

"They did see a woman that might be Ms. Kormer," he said. "It's hard to tell, Some of these hikers have been on the trail for a week or more, so they haven't had much chance to see the news."

I shrugged. "Better than what we had before, which was a great big steaming pile of nothing." I grabbed my pack, trying not to wince from the sore muscles I'd gotten from my daily workouts with Rade and the remaining psychological bruising from my adventure in the astral. "How far ahead is she?"

Joseph shrugged into his own pack. "Maybe a day," he said.

I nodded and strode onto the main trail. "Let's get going then. We're burning daylight."

•   •   •

I knew I was being childish, pouting over Joseph's insistence that I go back to the astral plane. I knew he was right, too. If I could get a grip on myself there, I'd be better able to manage my emotions during my sparring with Rade. I didn't care.

"Do it," he said, poking my leg with his toes. "Don't make me learn dream walking just so I can drag you from your dreams."

I rolled my eyes. "Whatever," I said. "Let's get this round of 'beat up Nicola' over with."

Joseph shook his head. "That's the spirit," he said dryly.

I closed my eyes and stepped into the astral for the half-dozenth time since my "vacation" had been interrupted. I knew I was going in half-afraid of the Fears, so it wasn't very surprising that one popped up quickly. What was surprising was how I reacted. A part of me was much more annoyed than afraid, and that part of me took over.

I dropped into my fighting stance and lashed out with a double punch before the Fear could do more than gape at me. It immediately dispersed in a damp, cold haze of black mist. I blinked at the spot where it had been in shock. A few more shades had begun to form, but quickly wisped away like smoke on the wind when I glanced at them.

I waited, feeling the muted awe in the back of my mind taking over any remaining fear I felt. After so many attempts, I had finally overcome the Fears.

"This is not what I expected to find."

I turned to Joseph and shrugged. "I guess my inner sulky teenager was just too emo to panic," I offered.

He laughed. "Okay, mistress of the astral, where to?"

I thought about it. We hadn't really planned for much outside of fighting off the Fears again, so I didn't really know what to do first. "Shall we look for Stella?"

Joseph nodded and held out his hands to me. I took them in mine and we closed our eyes to focus on the woman. There was a wavering feeling as we let our intent be known.

Searches in the astral could be tricky with more than one person. First of all, it took a lot of practice to find others in the astral plane, mainly because they appeared the way they saw themselves, not necessarily how they looked in their physical form. The many tricksters in the astral would sometimes interfere, posing as the person you were looking for just to mess with you. You had to be careful to know the energies you were looking for. Just identifying another mortal in the astral could be difficult.

Secondly, astral searches were about focusing your will and mind on a single idea. That was hard enough, but getting two people to focus on the same single idea was much harder. Each had their own perspective of what they were looking for, and any variations could cause problems.

Fortunately, Joseph had gotten most of his knowledge of Stella from my experience with her. We had talked about her while hiking and over the last few meals. And our years of experience working together with energy and magic made the attempt go much smoother. Joseph knew when to give me the control since I'd had more contact with the target.

If those obstacles could be overcome, the search was much more powerful. Despite my initial reluctance, I put on my professional hat and got to work. The wobbly feeling smoothed out, and I could feel the astral plane shifting around us, like a slight breeze.

A thought wandered through my mind: What if Jehovah/Satan tried something while Joseph was with me? The world suddenly shifted a different direction, and I gritted my teeth. We stopped, and I opened my eyes.

Joseph dropped his hands from mine and stepped away, staring around us in awe at Jehovah's garden. The cherry trees were in full bloom with fiery grasses blazing beneath them. The slate path was just as perfect as when I'd first seen it, going from koi pond to koi pond with a simple, stark beauty. Lilies flared up from the black of the water, colors mimicking the perpetual sunset framed by the mountains in the distance behind us.

"What is this?" Joseph breathed.

I grabbed his arm. "It's our cue to leave," I snapped. "This is Jehovah's garden."

CHAPT 11

Joseph's eyes widened, and he let me pull him around to face me. "You said Jehovah's garden was beautiful, but this..."

"Yup," I said. "A real heavenly place, if you know what I mean."

I clapped my hands onto Joseph's and squeezed his fingers. He was still staring around, and I could feel the pressure of time passing. Time in which we could be discovered here.

"You gotta close your eyes, Joseph," I reminded him. He hesitated, and I squeezed his fingers again to get his attention. "I don't want to face him right now. Please."

Joseph nodded, looking dazed. But his eyes fell shut, and I pulled back the focus I'd had on Stella before the stray thought had distracted me. The world tilted slightly, and I could feel the shift.

I opened one eye, half afraid I'd messed up again. Joseph was looking around with a slightly disappointed expression. Tall, well-trimmed bushes stretched out forming a corridor going to either side of us.

"A hedge maze," I said. "Great."

Joseph shrugged. "Them's the breaks. We should see what hints we can get from it though."

I put one finger along my cheek, propping my elbow on my other hand. "Hmm," I said, exaggerating the sound. "I wonder what the whole maze of plant-life could mean."

Joseph rolled his eyes. "I dunno," he said. "A gardening store?"

I smacked his shoulder and we laughed. "Which way?" I asked. "Left, right or up?"

"I say up," he said, after examining the other two directions carefully.

We kicked off and directed ourselves to float to the top of the hedges. Just as our heads came even with the top edge, the branches shifted and grew taller. We exchanged glances and tried again, with the same result.

"I don't think we get to do that," Joseph said.

"Yeah, back down we go."

We drifted back to the ground and peered down the paths between the hedges again.

"Split up?" he asked.

I nodded. "I'll take this way," I said.

Joseph headed the other direction, calling over his shoulder. "Back to the bodies at the first sign of trouble, okay?"

"Yup," I said, waving my hand behind me.

I trotted down the path, keeping an eye out for anything out of the ordinary. I almost laughed out loud at that, as if searching an illusory maze in a spirit realm for clues to the location of an escaped convict with magic items was anything close to ordinary, even for me.

I glanced back, unsurprised to see that Joseph was no longer behind me. I could still see along the path for hundreds of feet, but he was nowhere to be seen. I shrugged. It would have been a small comfort to see him, but that's how the astral plane works.

A small rustling noise caught my attention, and I skidded to a stop. I peered into the branches of the hedges, looking for the source of the sound. A small spotted skunk wriggled out of the leaves and squatted down, staring up at me.

"Hi," I said hopefully. "Can you help me?" I pictured Stella in my mind and sent it towards the creature. It sniffed the air for a moment as if tasting the thought, then it shuffled away.

I noticed the skunk musk as I followed, but it was light as if it had faded away. The skunk moved quickly, and I had to break into a jog to keep up. A small opening appeared in the hedges along one side, and the creature darted into it.

I crashed through the tiny space, branches and leaves clawing at my arms. The skunk was gone. A huge tree towered over me, roots exposed and clinging to the rocks around its base.

I stared in awe at the branches soaring in the air a hundred feet over my head. My eyes tracked down the trunk, covered with rough bark. The roots entwined across the granite and hung down in a curtain over a dark opening among the boulders.

I stepped forward tentatively and pushed the trailing roots aside. The cool air of the cave brushed against my face as I stepped inside. The darkness of the cave morphed into a soft glow in the air with a push of my will and desire.

I moved through the tunnels, hoping for a sign of Stella or the skunk, or anything else that could help me. Twice I tripped on roots arcing up from the floor of the tunnels. The second time, I reached out to the wall to catch myself and scraped my hand against the rough rock. Blood glistened against my palm, but I wiped it on my pants and kept moving.

I turned a corner and the tunnel opened into a large cavern. Stalactites and stalagmites lined the walls like the teeth of giant monsters. Quartz glittered in the rock walls, and water dripped rhythmically from somewhere I couldn't see. I moved through the space, shivering. My eyes darted around, latching on to each glint of light and shift of shadow. I rounded a large stalagmite and froze.

The creature before me stared with yellow eyes that flashed red in the shadows. Huge teeth filled an elongated jaw, and its fur flared in a ruff around its neck in shades of black. The beast lurched to its feet and shook itself out.

I finally remembered to breathe and air filled my lungs in a rush. The beast was hardly a wolf. Even calling it wolf-like was a stretch. But there was nothing else in my experience that would describe it so well. The legs were too long and thick, the tail too short. Its muzzle was longer, broader, and its teeth were just too much of everything. Too many, too big, too sharp, too deadly.

"You have a piece of Gleipnir," the creature said. Its mouth moved, but there was no way that movement created the words I heard. "You must be the hero."

It laughed, bitterness and disdain coloring the sound.

"You must be Fenrir," I choked out.

The creature grinned a not-quite wolfish smile. "I prefer Odin-Slayer," it said.

"I'm sure you do," I bit out. "I prefer The Bound One."

Fenrir snarled. "I'll not be bound long, hero! The mortal comes who will free me."

I shook my head. Shadows shifted in the corners of my vision, and I knew my fear was drawing the shadow creatures again. I prepared to step out of the astral. "I'll stop her," I said, trying to hide the tremor in my voice. "Stella will never free you."

The monster shook out its head, too short ears slapping against its skull. "Stop her, mortal," it laughed. "She is not my savior."

I gaped at the creature, trying to guess what it was telling me. "W-who-?"

Fenrir barked a laugh and lunged at me. Shadows rushed towards me. I choked on a scream and fled the astral plane.

CHAPT 12

"I warned you to leave at the first sign of trouble," Joseph called from the side.

I dodged a swing from Rade and snarled at him, "Yeah, I got it. I done screwed up." I lunged forward with a left-right combo.

Rade's icy eyes never left mine. "You engaged the wolf in the spirit realm. How is that possible?"

I rolled my eyes. "Am I the only one who remembers astral reflections 101?" I blocked a punch and Rade blocked my return blow. "It wasn't actually Fenrir." I ducked a high swing and thrust up with the heels of both hands at the Valkyrie's chin. She cocked her head at the last minute and the blow slid off her cheek. "He's been in the same place for so long, he's got an energy residue in the astral plane now."

"Like when there's certain animals that live in places for so long, a spirit guide is created in that same area," Joseph said. "See, I do remember."

I blocked a punch too late and took a glancing blow to the shoulder. "Good for you," I muttered.

Rade circled around me and I shifted my weight from one foot to the other, shuffling in place to keep myself facing her.

"So it's not the wolf," she said. "It's just an impression."

"Yeah," I said. "Like an after image." I blocked a blow and landed a solid hit to the Valkyrie's upper chest. "Since Fenrir is essentially immortal, it's very strong. It has a lot of his personality with it."

Rade nodded. "Makes sense," she said. Her body relaxed slightly, and I let some of the tension go in my own stance. "So why does he think you are going to free him?"

I dropped my hands and gaped at her. "What?"

She lunged forward and landed both fists on my chest. I felt the impact, then I was hit in the back by the planet.

"Oh, gods," I groaned, rolling over slowly. "Did you have to do that?"

Rade stood impassively over me. "I wasn't sure you'd considered the possibility," she said. "It was too good a distraction to pass up."

I rolled my eyes, my breath rasping in my throat. "Well, it worked," I mumbled.

Joseph appeared at my side to help me up. "It is a possibility," he said. "You could be the one Fenrir was talking about."

I scowled at him. "So could you," I pointed out. "I wouldn't be jumping on the blame bandwagon so quickly."

Joseph stared at me for a moment and then nodded. "Good point. It could be either of us. Or some other party that we haven't even met."

We turned to Rade, and she held up her hands. "It isn't me," she said.

I waved a hand at her. "Yeah, we know," I said. "Can't interfere. Will of Odin. Yadda yadda."

"It is a concern, though," Rade pointed out. "If what the astral Fenrir said is true, either Stella will pass the Runespell on to another, or one of you two will betray us."

I staggered over to the tea leftover from breakfast. "Gosh, Rade, you're such a messenger of hope and good times."

Rade frowned. "If you can't get your Berserker under control, how will you ever take on two people?" she asked.

I sipped my cold tea and sighed. "Not a clue," I said. "Not a damned clue."

Joseph sat next to me in silence for a few minutes before turning to me. "So, about that garden," he said.

I glanced up at him, then around the campsite. Rade was nowhere to be seen, so I assumed she'd taken off for the day. I grimaced and turned back to Joseph.

"Why didn't you want to be there?" he asked quietly.

I shrugged. "I've told you about the whole Satan and Jehovah thing before," I pointed out. "And dealing with him, er… them… whatever, is draining. Satan is so annoyingly vague and mysterious. Jehovah is a giant ball of ego." I sighed. "They are behind all of this, somehow, and they are trying to stop me."

Joseph watched me in silence. I knew I needed to admit it out loud, but it was hard to do it. There was so much pressure for me to stay strong and all that jazz, but the truth was, I was fragile and only a few hard knocks away from breaking.

"I'm afraid of them," I mumbled. "I know they can't directly hurt me, but they are divine beings, powerful beings." I sighed. "I'm standing up to them like I have a chance, but I'm just a mouse, squeaking valiantly at a snake about to strike."

Joseph moved, then, covering my hand with his. "I get it," he said. "These things… It seems like we never get a chance to just take a moment, but then we do and it's like, oh shit, did I say that to a *god?*"

I barked a laugh. "Yeah, and you know how my mouth can run."

Joseph patted my hand and stood up. "Well, it runs better than you can, sloth-girl."

I jumped up and scowled at him. "After all I've been through, I deserve better than that," I growled. "You can address me as sloth-woman."

•   •   •

I trudged behind Joseph, lost in my thoughts. I kept replaying the encounter with Fenrir, picking at each word, trying to find the meaning behind them. It was giving me a headache.

"Keep up, Nicola!" Joseph called.

I blinked and looked up. He had pulled several yards ahead of me and was watching me with an impatient look. I picked up the pace and caught up to him.

"I'm doing what I can to get you where you need to be," he said with a bite in his voice. "But you aren't helping with the feet dragging and the wool gathering."

I shrugged my shoulders, feeling defensive. Even though I understood why Joseph was acting the way he was, I couldn't seem to let his attitude slide off. "Fat lot of good it does me to get there if I have no clue what to do about it," I said. "I can't Berserk on command. I don't know who I'm stopping. I don't even know if I can make the decisions that I'm looking at having to make."

Joseph nodded, a hint of apology flashing across his face. "I know. And I haven't really helped with throwing doubt about you all over the place."

I barked a wry laugh. "Yeah, not so much."

Joseph sighed. "I do trust you, though," he offered. "Most of my doubt is out of fear. I mean, you have changed so much in the past few years, for good reason. But there it is. I've known you for nearly two decades, but you aren't who you used to be, and that terrifies me."

I shrugged. "I know, but it's necessary."

"I know," he said, stopping and facing me. "But I worry. Like I'm watching someone take up base jumping. It's probably okay, and I trust you, but it still hits me that it's a stupid move."

I nodded. "I get that. I wish it didn't have to be like this." I shifted my weight and sighed. "I mean, it's—"

"Don't move, Nicola," Joseph said in a tight whisper. "Gods, don't move."

I stared at him, but he was looking past my shoulder.

"What is it? Snake?"

He swallowed hard. "Cat. I think it's a cougar."

I nodded. "We should be okay, then," I murmured. "You're too old for her."

Joseph shot me a look. "Not a good time to be joking."

I nodded. "I'm going to turn slowly." I waited for his nod before I carefully shifted my feet rotating my body until I could peer into the trees and bushes behind us.

Crouching on a low branch, a lean, tan-colored feline stared at us. It was perfectly still, and the body language screamed that it was seriously considering attacking us.

"Damn," I said.

"Yeah."

A crazy thought hit me, and I acted before I could talk myself out of it. I unclipped the chest strap for my pack and slowly slipped it off my shoulders and down my arms.

"What are you doing, Nicola?" Joseph asked in a low, warning tone.

"How crappy would it be if, after all I've gone through, my quest ended in failure because of a stupid cat?" I asked mildly. "Random, stupid dangers all around, bringing down people who have survived real tragedies. World ends because a big kitty got a hankering for a couple of hikers."

I felt anger building in my chest as I focused on how unfair life could be. "My kids die in a fiery inferno caused by a bunch of religious nuts triggering Ragnarok and the world ending all because Mr. Wigglebutt there wanted a snack and we happened to come along."

"What are you doing?" Joseph hissed at me.

I stared at the cougar, letting it represent all the obstacles I'd been facing, all the unfair random things that kept me from doing the only thing I actually needed to do. My nose wrinkled and my brows drew down. I directed every frustration at it, focused every hiccup in my plans on it. The look of hate and anger deepened.

"Nicola?" Joseph hissed again.

"Get ready to run, Joseph," I said in a low snarl. "I'm actually getting angry now."

I heard him cussing behind me as my vision washed red, then yellow. I small grin flickered over the snarl, and I tensed my body, unconsciously mimicking the cougar's posture. I tried to think of some epic last words to cry out, but nothing came to mind except that rambling monologue by Rutger Hauer.

"Time to die," I crowed, and I leaped at the cougar.

CHAPT 13

In retrospect, I shouldn't have been able to make the jump. It was a good 10 feet up and at least 30 feet away. But that kind of logic wasn't even a shadow in my mind. My arms wrapped around the big cat as my abdomen slammed into the branch it was sitting on. It startled and tried to dodge, but apparently humans didn't fly at it howling with rage very often, and it was completely unprepared.

My grip on it pulled it down, despite its claws digging into the tree branch. I could feel the furry body twisting under my grasp and I swung my legs around it to keep it from moving me off its back. We landed in a crash of brush and snapping twigs, and my grip was knocked loose by the impact. I used the momentum to roll away and onto my feet, ignoring a burning pain in my side.

The cat got to its feet at the same time I did, and we faced each other. It tried to snarl at me, but my Berserker instincts assured me that its body language screamed fear. It was trying to bluff me.

I grinned and lunged at the cat, growling. I let the sigil burning on my chest take over my movements. I rolled under its high swiping claws, somersaulting along its side. I kicked out with my foot, hitting it in the face as it turned to follow me. The cat yowled, and gathered itself to pounce. I crouched down, ready for its attack. Instead, it leapt away, running through the brush away from the trail.

I sat there panting, staring after the cat for several minutes. Part of me was disappointed that the fight was over, but I wouldn't be able to catch it at a full run through the bushes.

My breath slowed, and the yellow faded from my vision. I stood up and rolled my shoulders. A pang in my side reminded me to check my body for injuries that might have been unnoticed in my adrenaline-fueled attack.

Fortunately, the mild pain only turned out to be a collection of scratches and bruises, with a single big bruise forming on my side bisected with a large scratch. I had probably hit a broken branch when I body-slammed the bough in my initial attack.

I made my way through the tangle of vines and branches and leaves back to the trail. I glanced back the way we'd come, and a wash of yellow fell over my vision for a moment. A deep green mist, like smoke or an energy trail, floated before me. I inhaled and smiled. Joseph. I turned to follow the scent up the trail the way we had been walking before Joseph had spotted the cat.

After a few yards, I rounded a small bend and found Joseph bouncing on his toes, watching the trail where I appeared.

"Nicola!" he cried and rushed up to me, dropping my pack at our feet before pulling me into a hug. "I thought for sure you'd be dead."

I grimaced, wincing when he pressed against the bruise on my side. "Not quite," I said. "I'm glad you ran, though. I'm not sure I could have stopped it if it had gone after you when it realized that I wasn't going down easily."

"You're okay, though?" he asked.

I showed him my bruise and let him do a quick antiseptic and a bandage on the scratch.

"Nothing else? You're sure?"

I nodded. "I think I scared the crap out of it attacking like that. It put on a bit of a show, then it just took off. It never even touched me."

He whistled. "That's lucky. Cat scratches are nasty things."

"I know," I said, shrugging my pack back on. "But in the meantime, we have a criminal to catch up to."

．　　　●　　　●

I lunged at Rade, trying to make contact. Instead, I over-extended myself and she landed a pulled blow to my ribcage. I could tell she pulled it. It only left a bruise instead of cracking a rib. I added that to the bruise on the other side from my fall with the cougar.

"Shit!" I panted.

Rade shook her head at me. "You are getting emotional," she said. "But you aren't Berserking. You are just making foolish decisions."

"That's me," I gasped. "Going the wrong way about it."

She rolled her eyes. "I was wondering if I was going to see the pity party today," she snapped.

I dropped my arms and gave her a look of disbelief. "What?"

"Excuses, whining, poor Nicola, 'I can't'..." she ticked off the points on her fingers. "You have an entire script of how you will never be able to do this."

"No, I don't," I scowled. I thought about what she said and tried to remember what I'd said during other training sessions. "I-I'm pretty sure I really don't."

"I thought you'd made a breakthrough yesterday."

"Me too. That cougar... it seemed so easy at the time."

"Perhaps that's because a cougar isn't the same as a person," Rade pointed out. "There isn't as much to face, and there isn't as much emotional and psychological risk."

I frowned, rolling my shoulders. "You mean, it isn't so much of a moral haze to chase off a cat than to cut the life thread of a real live person."

Rade sighed. "It doesn't matter," she said. "I think I've done all I can do to prepare you."

"Giving up on me already," I snapped, suddenly afraid and disappointed.

Rade shrugged at my tone of voice. "There's only so much I can do," she said. "I can try to get you there, but I cannot do it for you. I can train you, but I cannot learn it for you. I can tell you how the Berserker works, but I—"

"Can't Berserk for me?" I finished for her, the bitterness in my gut adding an extra bite to my words. "I get it. I have to do the work."

Rade shook her head. "That's not all of it, Nicola," she said, quietly. "We are running out of time, and you are running out of second chances."

I frowned at her as she heaved another sigh.

"I think it is time for me to return to the All Father," she said.

"You're giving up on me?" I couldn't keep the accusation from my voice.

"No," Rade said. "I must warn them to be ready."

"Ready?" I whispered. "For what?"

Rade turned her head, refusing to look at me. "I must tell them to watch for Fumbelwinter and the crowing of the red roosters."

My eyes widened. She was referring to signs that Ragnarok was beginning. "Oh gods," I moaned. "You *are* giving up on me! But, I can do this, I swear!"

Rade stared at me for a moment, then shook her head. "You say you can, but that is not good enough," she said. "Actions are what counts. It is time for me to leave you. You will do it or you will not."

My arms and legs felt numb as the shock of what she said washed over me, her words spinning in my mind. I choked on my words as the Valkyrie walked into the trees and out of sight.

"But I need your help," I whispered. "Don't I?"

•   •   •

I stumbled back to the camp to find Joseph humming over making tea. He glanced up at me and grinned. "I thought we'd fill our canteens with something hot to start off..." He trailed off when he noticed the shocked expression on my face.

"What's the matter, Nicola?" he asked moving quickly to my side.

"Rade," I muttered.

Joseph shot a look over my shoulder. "Rade? Is she hurt?"

"Gone," I choked out. "Left me."

He frowned and guided me to the log we'd been using as a seat. "Left you? Like, abandoned?" he asked. "I thought she was supposed to train you."

I took the tea that Joseph handed me and sipped it. It was too hot and my tongue prickled with the burn. "I failed," I said, taking a deep breath. "I am a failure. I couldn't do it. I couldn't make it happen. I couldn't, not even to save the goddam world."

"Again," Joseph offered.

I barked a laugh. "Yeah, again."

He stared at me as if I was missing something. I felt stupid for not seeing it, but I couldn't think of anything.

"What?" I finally asked.

"You don't get it," he said. "Again. You need to save the world again."

"Yeah. Like I said. So what?"

"This is - what? The third time?"

I shrugged. "So?" I said again.

Joseph frowned. "How many times do you need to save the world?" he asked. "How many times do you need to rescue all the people on this planet?"

I stared down at my tea, then knocked it back like a shot. "I don't know, Joseph. Until it's done? That's the deal I signed up for, remember?"

He shrugged. "It's a shitty deal," he said. "But you knew that, didn't you? You've known that for a while, and you didn't say anything because you didn't want anyone else to worry on your behalf."

I shrugged my pack on. "So?" I felt like a broken record.

Joseph rolled his eyes. "Dammit, Nicola. Just because you are the hero doesn't mean you tell the rest of the party to fuck off!"

I scowled. "What are you talking about?"

"It's like gaming, RPGs, tabletop."

I nodded. "Okay."

"You are the fighter-slash-wizard. Armor, magical powers, that kind of thing. You run into the dungeon first; you kill the bad guys."

"I'll buy that."

Joseph smirked. "But you can't just run off and leave the rest of the party. You're gonna want your healer-slash-priest. You'll want your thief. You'll want your barkeep who tells you where the cave full of monsters is."

I frowned, picking through the analogy he'd laid out. "And you think I'm ignoring my party?"

He nodded.

I chewed my lip, but Joseph's point didn't magically crystallize in my mind. I just didn't get what he was saying. Finally, I huffed. "Sweet baby Baldur, Joseph. I have no clue what you're talking about!" I realized I was shouting and toned down my volume. "You aren't making sense. You don't seem to realize that I don't have a party. It's just me."

Joseph gave me a sad look that somehow broke my heart and enraged me at the same time. I couldn't push past my frustration to follow his line of thought, and that frustrated me even more. His features blurred, and I realized tears were streaming down my face.

"Nicola, you are so stubborn," he muttered. I could hear the note of pleading in his voice. "Don't ignore us."

"Who?" I cried, flinging my arms out in emphasis. "Who am I ignoring?"

"Me," he said. "Hound Dog, Ames, Mercy, Rade, those cute Raven-men."

I laughed, bitterly. "You mean all the people I've dragged in to my own personal shit-storm up to now?"

Joseph shrugged. "You weren't exactly leaping in without a thought, yourself," he pointed out. "You were dragged. We were dragged. It's a drag. But once you got involved, you accepted a certain responsibility. Why do you insist on minimizing and dismissing the rest of us doing the same?"

"Yeah," I snorted. "I was made the 'hero of the quest'." I raise my hands in exaggerated air-quotes. "You guys didn't have that. You aren't obligated in that way."

"True," he said. "But we are your friends. We understand the situation when you bother to let us in on it. We can take a certain amount of responsibility on for ourselves because of that."

"Why would you do that?" I asked. "Why would you want it?"

"The four tenants of responsibility," he said. "To Know. To Will. To Dare. To Keep Silent."

"Those are the pillars of power," I pointed out.

"Yup," he said, grinning. "With great power comes great responsibility. To do stuff, or to Dare, gives us a responsibility. To will is to desire and energetically act on that desire. Also, responsibility. To keep silent is to monitor what we say and to who. Each choice we make to do that or not is a responsibility. And, lastly—"

"To Know," I murmured. "To have knowledge of something means you have to choose to do something about it or not. To share the knowledge or to act on it—"

"Or not," Joseph finished. "You are taking away our choice on that. Directly or not, you've given us the knowledge that this stuff happens, but you don't let us in on the details." He took my hands in his. "You don't have that right, to choose for us."

I felt my face flush. "I didn't think about it like that," I said.

"Of course not," Joseph agreed cheerfully. "That's why I get to call you on it."

I scowled at him and he grinned back.

"Are we done being all mushy now?" I grumbled.

"Are you going to think about what I've said?"

I sighed, putting a bit more drama into it than I actually felt. "Yes, fine."

"Okay, then," he said. "Let's hit the trail."

CHAPT 14

I followed Joseph as he led me out of the woods again. I was thankful he'd studied up on the Appalachian Trail before this little trip, since I had no idea what to look for or where to find camping spots or resupply stops. We needed supplies, and we needed information. Therefore, we were stopping at a little grocery and gas station just off the trail.

Still, I wasn't happy. It was time I didn't think we could afford to spare, even though I knew, logically, that we wouldn't get far if we didn't eat. Logic wasn't behind the near panic that drove my legs faster and farther each day.

We trudged up the dirt path that spilled into the huge gravel parking lot. People could park their cars there before hitting the Trail for a day or two. There were several storage buildings and ramshackle sheds behind the grocery, and a small ancient sheet-metal mobile home sat at the edge of the clearing.

I wrinkled my nose at the hot dust that rose up in the slight breeze. It was much warmer out in the open than it had been in the shelter of the trees. We stepped onto the wooden porch of the store and Joseph held the door open for me. I ducked into the slightly cooler air and let my eyes adjust before I headed further into the store.

It was a tiny building, more like a convenience store than a grocery. The ceiling was low and there were several fluorescent lights burned out or flickering weakly, with the annoyingly vague hum that came with the poor lighting. The tile floor was grubby, like it was too old to ever look clean. A stale smell floated up from the shelves, and I made a mental note to check shelf-life dates.

A low irritating thrum came from the wall of coolers along the back. It wasn't the normal hum those coolers put out. It sounded more like they were on their last leg, groaning with the effort of keeping half-gallons of milk from spoiling.

As I adjusted to the air inside, I quickly realized that the coolness was only slight, and more likely from the fans placed in each corner of the store than from any kind of AC unit. I stopped and waited for Joseph. "Let's hurry up and get out of here," I muttered. "What's on the list?"

He watched me for a long moment then said, "Why don't you go quiz the cashier about our escapee while I get our supplies."

I nodded and headed for the front of the store again. This time, I noticed the tightly packed racks of books, bumper stickers, t-shirts and other swag, all loudly proclaiming a very conservative and very Christian narrative. I sighed and hoped it wasn't a sign of the interaction I was about to have.

I don't have a problem with conservatives or Christians, but I've found that the combination usually makes for someone who is hostile and aggressive, either because I'm too dark on the complexion spectrum for their taste, too female for their respect, or too Pagan for any conversation other than how much I was going to their Hell.

I smiled and wondered what that type would do if I told them Hel owed me one and Jehovah was the littlest bit scared of me. Both technically true, not that I'd ever want to actually push those particular gods on either point.

The guy at the cash register was a bit older than me, with a dusty, surly look and a MAGA hat perched on his thinning hair. I had to give him credit though. What he was losing on his head, he was letting go wild on his chin. I smelled old dirt and motor oil coming off of him, or at least off of his coveralls, which looked more like he just never washed them than that they had been dirtied by "honest" hard work.

I smiled at him, putting on my nice people face. He gave me what might have been a toothy grin back, except he was missing quite a few of the teeth. I took a deep breath and steeled myself for what was sure to be an uncomfortable conversation.

"Hi," I said, forcing my voice to be cheerful. "I was wondering if you'd seen someone pass by here. Someone hiking the trail?"

The man huffed and turned his attention back to the small TV behind the counter. "See a lot of folks here hiking the trail."

I nodded. "I bet. I'm talking about a woman. She would have been alone." I could see that the guy wasn't planning on being very helpful, but I pressed on, hoping for the best. "She's about 40ish years old, a little shorter than me. She's got short, dark blonde hair, and she was wearing an army-green coat and gray backpack last time I saw her."

The man's eyes flicked to my face and narrowed before going back to the TV. I held my breath, hoping that was a good sign. The man watched a truck commercial with interest, working his jaw like he was chewing something.

The commercial ended and he turned back to me, picking up a stack of brochures for local businesses. "Seems I might have had someone come in with that description," he muttered. "Could be I got some video surveillance." He drew out the last two words like they were a bit more high up on the vocabulary rating than he was used to using.

I clenched my hands together trying to hold back my excitement. "When was she here?"

"Dunno," he said. His eyes were locked on his hands as they tapped the brochures into straight lines along all four sides before starting the cycle again. "Coulda been yesterday or the day before. Video has dates, though."

"Would you be able to check?" I asked, desperation leaking into my voice.

"Nah," he said. "Gotta watch the store."

I slumped in defeat.

"But you could go watch em," he added, his eyes flicking back to the TV. A monster truck rally was advertising a local event with loud announcer voices and funny names flashing in a staggering array of fonts for each of the vehicles.

"Oh, thank you!" I said.

The man pointed out the back door to the mobile home. "They're out there. Billy should be there. Just tell him what you told me."

I shot a glance over my shoulder at Joseph. He was still busy filling out his list, peering intently at the sparsely filled shelves. "Could you let my friend know where I've gone?" I asked, heading for the back door.

"Yup," he said, waving his hand over his head. He was fixated on the scantily clad women promoting some kind of gum on the TV.

I shook my head at the man, who seemed a few sandwiches short of a picnic on both intellect and attention span, and trotted out the door, hoping I wouldn't take too long with this. The mobile home was just as run down as I'd initially thought. Large rust patches showed where the pale blue and mint green paint had flecked and faded.

I jogged around the structure to the door and knocked briskly. A skinny version of the man in the grocery opened the door.

"Whatcha want?"

"Hi," I said. "The man in the store said to talk to you about watching a video?"

The guy frowned in disbelief, and I rushed on, hoping he wouldn't turn me away from our best lead in days. He seemed a bit more focused than the other man, and I hoped he would be more sympathetic.

"I'm looking for a woman who passed through, no more than a few days ago. I really need to find her." I rattled off the description again, and the man's face changed from a scowl to surprise, then his mouth curved into a friendly smile.

"Oh, ok," he said. "Get separated from a friend or something?" He held open the door, and I bounced up the steps.

"Something like that," I said. "I just really need to know if she came this way."

The man waved me down the narrow space between the stove and some built-in cabinetry. "All the way back," he said. "Gotta keep those videos safe, you know."

I walked back, shrugging off the tension that sprang up on the back of my neck and between my shoulders. I stepped into the small room at the end of the hallway and looked around for a TV or something.

There was a small bed and some built-in drawers and tiny cabinets, but nothing that looked like what I could watch security videos on. Fear sprang into my gut and my vision washed over with yellow. I frowned, blinking rapidly to clear it. Now was not the time to be going violent on some random guys.

I shook my head and backed a step out of the room. "I don't see—"

A sharp pain exploded in my head, and everything went black.

• • •

I immediately knew I was dreaming. I was caught in a kaleidoscope of images.

A spotted skunk waited for me at the end of a forest path. I ran towards it, but a cougar leapt at me from a tree that stretched hundreds of feet into the air. I ducked under it and ran into the cave hidden by the tree's roots. I climbed through the tunnels until I reached a rusty old mobile home.

I ran up the steps and into the mobile home to find Jehovah's garden, dripping with mold and decay. Koi floated, dead, in the ponds in between dried up lilies. I turned and ran back to the gate of the garden. Satan laughed with glee, and I turned to look over my shoulder, searching for him. I turned back and found Fenrir snarling at the garden gate.

I veered to the side and jumped over a garden bench, landing in fiery grasses. I waded through the grass, and the plants grew and became a deeper green until I was running along the hedge maze.

"Joseph!" I called out. My voice left my mouth in a whisper. I couldn't push past the lump in my throat no matter how hard I tried.

Rade stepped in front of me and I slid to a stop, falling on my butt at her feet. She scowled down at me, and she changed into the kind but firm face of Odin, his false eye not quite right.

"You cannot fail," he intoned.

"I know," I cried. "I'm trying!"

"You cannot fail," he said again. "But you will not win."

He pulled away, and I scrambled to my feet, reaching out for him. "What do you mean?"

"He means you'll never make it out alive," said a voice behind me.

I spun around and found Tyr shaking his head at me, and expression of deep sorrow on his face.

"We never make it out alive," he said.

A noise clattered behind me, and I whipped my head around to find the grocery clerk grinning at me. He morphed into Jehovah and spoke. "You don't even know what you've gotten yourself into, my child."

I watched as he grew larger, angry at me for knowing too much. Pain exploded in my head and I fell to my hands and knees. Rough hands grabbed me and lifted me up. I tried to struggle, but I couldn't move.

My vision was clouded by the pain, but I felt myself dropped into a chair. Rough bonds wrapped around my waist and wrists, holding my arms in place with my hands together behind my back, the back of the chair digging into my elbows. I felt hands move my feet, and my ankles were tied to the chair legs.

Panic flooded my mind, bitter acid burning up the back of my throat. I tried to move, to tug at the bonds, but my muscles were limp and refused to respond to my will. Tears burned behind my eyes as pain and hopelessness filled me.

I tried to listen for something, but there was nothing to hear. The emptiness filled my ears with a muted white noise roar. I tried to whimper, just to see if I could still hear, but my voice was no more at my command than my limbs.

An eternity passed in the silence.

CHAPT 15

A loud banging noise startled me. I jerked my head up from where it had been lolling against my chest. I winced at the ache in my neck and head. I blinked my eyes rapidly and stared up at the men, nearly identical, except one was older and had more weight on his frame. I dazedly wondered if they were brothers or father and son.

The two men stared at me with identical cold, calculating gazes, and I realized they were probably a bit more intelligent than I'd first assumed. Figures I'd be done in by stereotyping a group of people. The irony of that brought laughter bubbling up my throat, and I swallowed dryly to keep it down.

The older man stepped forward, still staring at me. "You'll never catch her."

It took me a moment to realize he'd meant Stella Kormer. I scowled. "What do you care?"

He smiled an unpleasant grimace. "The work of the Lord is what I care about, heathen," he said. "We obey the word of God, and He has spoken to us."

"Amen!" the younger man called out.

The older man nodded, glancing at back at Billy. "We have been blessed to receive special orders from our Lord."

"Praise be to God!"

"Praise be His word," the man continued, looping his thumbs around the straps of his coveralls. "For He spoke of the woman you seek." He leaned in close to me. "And He spoke of the whore who would pursue her."

His eyes ran down my body, lingering over my breasts and thighs. I suppressed a shiver as he sneered down at me. After a long, terrifying moment, he stepped back a few paces.

Billy had moved around to stand behind me while I was focused on the creepy older man. His voice took up the narrative. "The good Lord bade us capture the wolf who hunts his flock! And we are pleased to obey!"

"Hallelujah!" the older man crowed.

I felt the younger man's hands rest on my shoulders. I immediately flashed to Zaro and panic choked me. My vision went hazy with the fear pulsing through me. This couldn't be happening again. But how could I fight it? I wasn't even sure if I meant the anxiety-driven fears or the possibility of being assaulted. It didn't matter. The Berserker was still something I couldn't seem to call up when I needed it. My hands were, literally and figuratively, tied.

"What are you going to do with me?" I finally choked out.

The younger man leaned down behind me, sliding his hands along my arms. "I'm sure you already know that, whore," he whispered.

His hand slipped under my shirt and his fingers slid down into the waistband of my pants. I squeezed my eyes shut, and tried not to focus on him fumbling at the elastic waist of my underwear.

"We wait for the Lord to tell us," the older man said firmly.

I opened my eyes as Billy pulled his hands away from my body and stepped around me. The older man and Billy stared at each other.

"She's a whore," Billy said after a moment. "God said so."

The older man shook his head. "For a whore is a deep ditch, boy. Don't be caught by the temptation."

Billy frowned. "All sins be forgiven—"

The older man cut him off. "No whoremonger, nor covetous man, who is an idolater, hath any inheritance in the kingdom of Christ and of God." He shook his head. "Don't throw away your soul for such things, Billy."

The younger man scowled. "Fine." He stalked out the door, throwing a look at me over his shoulder.

I knew he'd be back to do what he wanted when the older man wasn't watching him. I choked back a sob and turned my eyes on the older man. He stared at me with almost no expression on his face, like I was a bit of scrap metal that he wasn't sure he wanted to salvage or just toss. I tried not to squirm in my chair while he stared at me.

"Don't you even want to know why I'm trying to find Stella?" I asked finally, the silence driving me to speak.

The man's eyebrows twitched. "Who?"

I frowned. "Stella," I repeated. "Stella Kormer. The woman I was asking about?"

He shrugged. "Doesn't much concern me," he said. He lifted a hand when I moved to speak again. "I don't question God. He has His reasons for why this... Stella should be helped, and why you should be stopped."

He reached into his pocket and pulled out a bottle of water. "He said to stop you, and we stopped you," he murmured, holding the bottle so I could take a few gulps. "Makes no difference to me. If the good Lord says to kill you tomorrow, I will. But He said stop you, so we gonna have to wait until He tells me what's next."

My eyes widened at his words and I simply stared at him as he walked to the door.

He stopped and turned before he left. "I let your friend know where you were," he said. "Just like you asked." He grinned at my confused expression. "Told him you asked about that woman, that you got your information and took off. Told him I didn't see where you went to."

I slumped in the chair, my shoulders sagging in defeat. Joseph probably thought I'd ran off into the woods on my own, or maybe that I'd gotten a lead to follow Stella into town. How could I know what conclusions he'd drawn from that?

The man chuckled a bit and walked out.

"Great," I said to myself. "A crazy fundie with a hotline to Jehovah and his equally crazy mini-me." I tugged my hands against the ropes, but they were solid. "Why not? Bob was crazy. Nancy was crazy. Jehovah was a great big package of cuckoo puffs."

I lashed out with my feet, trying to loosen the ropes around my ankles. Nothing. "And me? I'm just a useless idiot running into the crappy mobile homes of random rednecks, 'cause why not? Now I'm stuck here, talking to myself."

Finally, I'd exhausted my attempts to free myself. I stared around the small building. It was probably one of the storage sheds I'd seen behind the grocery, but I couldn't tell for sure.

Sunlight streamed in through hairline cracks in the walls and through a large hole in the roof only about 10 feet off the ground. The irregular circle left a blinding yellow-white patch on the ground about two feet away from me. The light showed the dust motes flying thickly through the air, giving me an idea of how seldom the building was used.

It looked like the building was just sheet metal over a sparse wooden frame. The door was metal also with a handle that looped out from the warped steel. It looked like it didn't have a latch, so I figured it probably padlocked on the outside.

A rustling noise drew my attention, and I noticed a large rat running along the base of one of the walls. I bit my lip. Rats weren't a good sign. These weren't the pet store kind of animals. These were the opportunistic scavenger type. And a tied-up person was just the kind of opportunity they would take advantage of.

I needed to get out of here before Billy or the rat could take their own little piece of me.

•　　　•　　　•

I'd never been able to dream walk, but I'd known some people who told me how it worked. If I had understood them correctly, I would be able to get to some kind of dream world portal in the astral plane. Then, I'd just have to figure out which of the billions of dreams was Joseph's and try to navigate it well enough to give him my location.

No problem, right?

The sun had set a while back, and I hoped it was late enough for Joseph to be asleep. I shot a glance at the door and then at the last place I'd seen Ratty. It looked like the coast was clear, so I figured it was time to give it a shot. I didn't exactly have the luxury of waiting much longer.

I stepped into the astral plane, ignoring the jumpiness in my gut. It was now or never for me to get over my astral issues. I glared at a dark shape that started to form near me, and it faded away.

I nodded my head sharply and closed my eyes. I pictured the closest thing to a dream world I could think of, focusing more on the idea than the image. I pushed at my will and let the emotions of my desperation feed into it.

I felt the slight shift and opened my eyes.

CHAPT 16

"Wow!" I breathed.

My surroundings were dark blue-black like deep water. Everywhere I looked there were glowing shapes. They speckled the darkness as far as I could see in every direction.

They glowed in every color imaginable. Bright white, fiery red, cool blue, passionate magenta, sickly pea green. I even saw darker inky blobs against the dark blue ocean of the dream world.

Some were round, some oval, some asymmetrical, like an amoeba. Some had tails or tendrils, some had spikes. As I watched them, the shapes would change. I could almost hear a *blurp-blurp*, as if they were bubbles morphing in a viscous liquid.

I reached out to a nearby blob, a healthy green shade with feathery edges. Before my hand could even touch it, I could feel the emotions of the dream wash over me. It was a happy dream, about a camping trip with family.

I pulled my hand back, suddenly aware that touching a dream might get me sucked in to random dreams. At the very least, that was time I didn't have to waste. I closed my eyes again, ready to try for Joseph's dream. I latched on to the image of the dream world, overlaying it with my emotions and impressions of Joseph. I felt a small lurch and opened my eyes.

A dream floated just in front of me, inches from my nose. It was a deep royal blue oval that seemed comfortable somehow. I lifted my hand and tried to sense the energy of the dream. I smiled at the emotional energy I felt. It was definitely Joseph's dream. It felt like him, like his energy, like the brush of his mind when we worked together in spell casting.

I took a deep breath. This was the hard part. After all, the dreamer controlled the dream, so I would risk being trapped or overwhelmed by whatever the dream was. I was pretty good at lucid dreaming, which meant I could consciously control and perceive my own dreams. I'd developed the skill years ago, but I usually let my dreams go how they would so I could learn from them.

Dreams could tell you things about what was going on in the world around you. Dreams could put things into patterns and understanding in ways that the conscious mind would never come up with, and I could use that to see my own life path more clearly. Of course, that didn't mean I always enjoyed my dreams, but enjoyment wasn't the goal.

Dream walking was about lucid dreaming on the perceptual end of things but in someone else's dream. Just like in your own dream, you could be sucked in to what was going on. But other people's minds were always just a bit alien, and that added extra danger to the experience.

I glanced around at the other dreams floating around me and let my mind wander a bit. I knew I was avoiding taking the next step, but I was also finding the dream world fascinating. The dream world was kind of on the edge of reality. Dreams could be a portal to the astral, just as the astral plane could be a portal to the dream world and even Dreamtime.

Dreamtime was a whole other level of existence. It overlapped the dream world in the sense that all dreams were a part of Dreamtime and Dreamtime was all dreams. But it was more than that.

Dreamtime was a kind of shared dream, not just of all people but of all things. It was overlaid with the real world, and it was overlaid with the dream world and all the dreams in it. But it also was something different.

In a way, it was the dream of the entire planet... or maybe the universe. It was a reflection of reality that showed what was, what could be, what had been before, and what was coming. It also brought to life all the dreams, nightmares, and desires of each being that contributed to it.

I had brushed against Dreamtime once or twice in my past, and I knew I was nowhere near ready to try making my way in the full Dreamtime plane. Perhaps, someday, I would find the courage to approach the Rainbow Serpent, ruler of Dreamtime, and begin what would be a lifetime or more of learning to walk Dreamtime.

I sighed. That wasn't going to happen now. I had a schedule to keep and not much energy to spare for that kind of thing. I looked at Joseph's dream again and, before I could hesitate again, I reached out my hand towards the blue egg floating before me, and touched it.

•   •   •

I was falling. The wind blew past my ears, cold and whistling. My arms reached for something to grab on to, but there was nothing. It was just falling. I waited for the ground to rush up to meet me, but there was nothing. So I just kept falling.

I lurched forward like something had yanked the world sideways, and I was walking down a dark hallway. My footsteps rang out, echoing in the pitch black. I stopped for a moment, listening for any other sound. After a moment, footsteps sounded ahead of me. The echoes made it impossible to determine how far, so I jogged, my arms stretched in front of me in the black.

The floor dropped out from beneath me, and I was in a jungle, pushing my way through plants and vines that squished under my touch. I looked at my hands and saw they were covered with paint as if my surroundings were made of colored oils.

"Joseph," I called. "You've seen that movie too many times."

I heard a rustling noise ahead of me, and I pushed forward with a burst of energy. A vine fell across my neck, and I tried to push through the paint like the rest of the plants. Instead, it looped around my neck and waist, and lifted me off my feet. The vine hissed at me, and I saw that it was a snake of some kind.

I could hear squishing footsteps as if someone was coming up behind me.

Joseph poked his head around a tree. "Oh, Nicola," he said. "There you are."

I gurgled at him, flailing my arms.

He shook his head at me, crossing his arms over his chest. "This is what you get for running off without me." He looked around. "Now where is this supposed to be?"

I gurgled again, trying to pull myself up so I could breathe.

"Well, it's the woods, for sure," he muttered. He peered up into the sky. "Sunny, so... south? But we came from that way."

I kicked out with my feet, nearly hitting Joseph's arm. He blinked up at me and frowned.

"You don't have to be like that, Nicola," he said. "I'm trying to find you." He turned away. "Maybe I should go to the astral plane to find you."

I kicked out again and felt the snake's coils slip. I lashed out before it could tighten them back up and I slipped down so that the snake was holding me around my head and cheeks instead of my neck.

"Jo'sheth!" I cried, my cheeks pressed together and my jaw locked by the pressure of the snake's coils. "Sheh! Ko'shry! Helll!"

The pressure released suddenly, and I was back in the dream world. I shook my head to clear it, then looked around for Joseph's dream. It was nowhere to be seen. I closed my eyes and searched for it that way, but nothing happened, and I opened my eyes to the same dreams that had surrounded me when I'd closed them.

"Dammit," I muttered. The only explanation was that the dream had ended, which meant that Joseph had either woken up or stepped into the astral plane. Either that or I simply wasn't able to find his dream this time.

I shook my head, dismissing that. I simply couldn't fail that badly again. If I did, I was going to likely die. I stepped into the astral plane and searched for Joseph there. I had no success with that any more than finding Joseph's dream again. I tried searching for the ravens, hoping they could send Joseph or Rade a message. But they weren't around either.

"So much for that," I muttered. "Joseph thinks I'm abandoning my party, but here I am. I can't find a damn single one of you when I need you."

I sighed, knowing my anger was half-hearted. I didn't blame them for not being around. I was just as much to blame for being on my own as anyone else. And making snotty comments to myself in the astral plane was about as useless an action as I could come up with. The best I could hope for was that Joseph had gotten my message somehow and woken up. I shook my head wearily and stepped back into my body.

CHAPT 17

I dozed fitfully all night, startling at every sound. I was sure that every rustle and creak was the rat coming to nibble at my toes or Billy coming for something more. My eyes and throat both burned from the dust and lack of sleep. My arms and legs burned with lack of movement. My butt was sore from being in the same position on it for so long.

When the older man walked through the door sometime after the light started showing through the cracks in the walls, I was nearly relieved to see him. He gave me more water and, after I wheedled for a moment, he untied me so I could relieve myself in a bucket. He turned his back on me, warning me not to try anything, but I could barely move enough to squat over the bucket, never mind attempting to kick his heavy-weight ass.

He leaned over me to tie me up again. "I'm gonna be praying for ya, missy," he said. "The good Lord's gonna tell me what to do with you. I hope He says you can be forgiven."

He nodded to himself as he walked to the door.

"Tell him hi from Nicola," I ground out. "Tell him I stopped by the garden, but he wasn't there."

The man looked back at me with a confused look on his face.

I grinned weakly. "I mean, we didn't really part ways on friendly terms last time," I admitted. "But I was trying to stop him from ending the world, so..." I shrugged.

"You saying you talk to the Lord our God?" the man said, a scowl on his face.

"Yeah," I said. "I keep undermining his plans, so I wouldn't say we get along or anything."

The man snorted. "Liar," he said. "The likes of you cannot stop the Great

Almighty."

I barked a laugh. "Tell him that," I said. "He seems to be pretty upset that I keep doing it. That's why he had to send you after me."

The man frowned. "It is an honor to serve the Lord, but don't think He needs our help."

I grinned. "Then why doesn't he do it himself?" I asked. "Wait, no, I know this one! He's testing you, right?" I nodded. "He's always testing his followers. It's like, he's God, but he would really rather be a high school teacher."

"Your words are blasphemous!"

"Yeah," I admitted. "But the thing is, he's got a million and one ways to test you. He could ask you to pray to him at 3:05 in the morning every day for a year. That would test dedication like nothing else. He could ask you to sacrifice Billy or find a sacred something or other. But no. He asked you to do a job that he should be able to do himself." I shrugged. "It just seems a little suspicious."

The man shook his head. "It ain't for us to know the mind of the Lord." He smiled at me with a look of compassion. "And I will pass on your words to Him."

I smirked. "If he ever bothers talking to you again," I called as the man shut the door behind him.

"Great," I muttered. "Trussed up like a goose and grasping for verbal insults to throw at some guy with a 3rd-grade vocabulary." I sighed. "Some hero I turned out to be."

"Our favorite," a familiar voice said.

I whipped my head around. "Huginn! Muninn! Gods, I'm glad to see you!"

The two large black birds hopped around me, eyeing me from all sides.

"Quite a fix," Muninn said.

"A fix you're in," agreed Huginn.

"Yeah," I said. "And it's teetering on the edge of being even worse. I need you guys to get Joseph for me."

Huginn clacked its beak while Muninn shook out its feathers.

"Don't know if we can," Muninn said after a moment.

"Might break rules," Huginn replied.

"What rules?" I cried.

"Might be interfering," Huginn said gently.

"Cannot interfere," confirmed Muninn.

I sighed, frustration building. "You can't help me because it would be interfering? Then why are you here?"

"No, no, no," Huginn said.

"Can help," Muninn echoed.

"Can you untie me?" I asked.

The ravens shook themselves in unison.

"We are messengers," Muninn said.

I huffed out a breath. "Yeah, I know—"

"We can give information," Huginn interrupted.

I scowled. They had never interrupted me like that before. The two had been much more helpful in the past, and it was pissing me off. It was like something had changed since the first time I'd met them.

There was the time I'd spent in the Center, but they had simply given me support, and some sandwiches. I smiled wryly at the memory of that. I guessed that if I asked for some food, they would gladly deliver, but I didn't want to be stuck here so long that I was at risk of starving.

I thought back to when I'd met them in the astral plane. I had been feeling hopeless, trying to find clues to where Joseph and I had sent the Runespells after we'd managed an actual hiding spell just before being captured by good ol' Bob.

The two had shown up and given me some riddle-like hints at what they could do for me. Eventually, I worked out that they could give me sensory memories that would help me find the pendants. It had been a painful process to get the memories, and nearly as much to sift through them to get anything I could work with.

I shook my head. Huginn and Muninn seemed to like me, in general, and they wanted me to succeed as much as any of the Norse gods and god-creatures. So, why would they hold out on me now?

Unless they weren't. The thought drifted into my mind, and I frowned. Maybe I was expecting the wrong things.

Before they had spoken in riddles. Now, I was trying to get them to come out and say what they could do for me. But, if they were just talking the same way they always had, then I could assume they had given me all the clues I needed to figure out what they were telling me.

"You can't do what I asked you to do," I said slowly. "Because that would be interfering."

The birds stopped snapping their beaks playfully at each other and looked at me, heads cocked to the side.

I bit my lip, trying to remember my exact words. "I asked you to bring Joseph to me, didn't I? And you can't do that."

"Clever Nicola," Huginn said.

Muninn bobbed its head. "Keep thinking!"

"But you can help me," I said. Then it hit me. "You are messengers!" I cried. "Can you give Joseph a message from me?"

Muninn stretched up, flapping its wings. "Yes! Yes!"

Huginn hopped over to stand directly in front of me. "Tell us what to say!"

I let out the breath I'd been holding. "Tell him I'm being held prisoner in one of the sheds behind the grocery. Tell him I didn't run off without him."

Huginn and Muninn hopped a few feet away.

"And please," I said. "Hurry!"

The ravens sent me a look that somehow reassured me, then they stood side by side, and turned back to back, disappearing as they rotated.

CHAPT 18

I jerked awake, the sound of the door squealing open wrenching me from my fitful dozing. I blinked my eyes, trying to focus in the near pitch-black of the shed at night.

"Who's there?" I mumbled.

Hands grasped at me, fumbling at the ropes. It took me a moment to realize they were untying me.

"Joseph?" I whispered. "Is that you?"

The ropes around my waist fell away, and the hands fumbled at my ankles.

"Thank the gods you're here," I hissed. "We need to hurry!"

The hands finished with the ropes and grasped my arms, pulling me to my feet and away from the chair. It took a few seconds for me to realize that the grip was too rough and the man too short for it to be Joseph.

"What—"

I was pulled close to the man, and he held me with one arm, clapping the other rough hand over my mouth. After a brief, feeble struggle on my part, Billy wrestled me to the ground, pinning me down with his body. I tried to scream and kick, but being tied to a chair for two days had weakened me, and my legs cramped up when I tried to use them to fight the man off.

His hand pressed against my mouth and along my shoulder, effectively pinning down my head and arm. His other hand ran along my body, squeezing at my breasts and hips roughly through my clothes. He ground his pelvis into my groin, and I struggled not to break down in tears.

I tried to focus on my hate like I'd done with Zaro, but every pinch and grope sent tremors of fear through me. Nausea flowed through my gut in wave after wave. I half hoped I would vomit on him, though I was pretty sure there was nothing in my stomach to vomit. He started thrusting his hips against me, grinding rhythmically through our pants. I tried to kick him away again, without success. After a few moments, he let out a long groan and collapsed on top of me, panting.

I froze, terrified and confused. Then he started murmuring in my ear, his acrid breath turning my stomach even more.

"Not s'posed to give in," he said. "I'm s'posed to fight temptation. I'm s'posed to wait." He grabbed my breast hard. "I have to wait for some righteous woman," he growled. "I have to wait to marry someone worthy. But they all show themselves to be whores. So I have to wait. I can't lay with a whore, but I can't find a wife, so I have to wait."

It hit me, what he was saying. "Are you a-a virgin?" I asked, mumbling around his loosened fingers.

He pinched my nipple hard. "Don't you make fun," he warned.

"No, no!" I said. "I wouldn't." His grip relaxed, and he let his other hand slip away from my mouth. "Is the other man your father?"

Billy nodded.

"And he decides the women you want to marry are whores?" I guessed.

"I been tryin' for a wife for 15 years," he said. "I'm sick of waiting."

"I can imagine," I assured him. "It not fair."

He propped himself up, as if staring at me in the dark, though I doubted he could see me much better than I could see him.

"It's not fair," he agreed.

I took a deep breath. It looked like my best chance was to appeal to him as a sympathizer to his situation. I wasn't sure how to go about doing that though. "I wish I could help," I offered.

"You can," Billy whispered.

I swallowed. "Oh?"

"Are you a whore?" he asked.

"N-no!" I choked out. I certainly didn't want him to think my body was available for his use.

"Good," he muttered, lifting up my shirt to expose my basic white sports bra. "Then you can be my wife."

I froze in shock, realizing the direction his thoughts had taken. His hands were fumbling with my zipper before the full implications finally clicked in my mind. Just as quickly, I was back at the Center, crippled by the feelings forced into my mind by the Runespell Zaro used to pacify his wives. I could feel the confusion of wanting to go back because of the feelings, but knowing I was being violated at the same time.

My limbs fell limply as wet lips moved across my mouth and down my neck, and I couldn't tell if they were Billy's or Zaro's. I couldn't think, I couldn't move. I could barely breathe.

Then, somewhere in my mind, I heard a screaming sound. I focused on it, trying to figure out where it came from. It was a horrible twisted sound, like a mixture of a woman's screech, a child's scream, and a retching cry.

It was the monster.

Inside all of us is a monster. It is all the negative thoughts, doubts, failures, and flaws we hold about ourselves. It is the thing we must face to grow, but it is a disgusting, wretched creature.

I faced the monster at the Center when I was trying to get past the things that had happened. If I was being honest with myself, I had only taken the first step. I hadn't done any of the follow-up work that would have made facing the monster more effective.

Now, I was immobilized by the feelings I still had, the fears and the guilt and the hate, about what Zaro had done. Because I knew that on some level, I had let it happen. I had sworn to the monster, and the child it had morphed into, my inner child, that I wouldn't let it happen again.

But here I was. And the monster was screaming the betrayal.

"No," I whispered.

Billy shifted, moving his body off of mine so he could pull my pants down over my hips.

"No," I said louder, and time froze.

My vision washed over with yellow, giving the darkness a green tint. I felt my eyes change, relaxing like when I was looking with my aura sight. But it wasn't aura sight. I felt my pupils elongate, then open wide. An odd sensation washed over the backs of my eyeballs, and suddenly, the light was enough to see by.

Billy hovered over me, his hands at the waistband of my jeans, a confused look on his face. A thought floated in the back of my mind that he'd honestly thought I would agree to marry him.

The pendants hanging on the chain around my neck felt cold against my skin, except for one. It burned hot on my flesh, and the song of protection rasped out of my throat. I wrenched at my aching muscles, bringing both knees nearly up to my chin. My feet came together in front of Billy's chest and I kicked out, sending him flying.

I swung my legs around in a circle, twisting my body to use the inertia to get to my feet. I launched myself at the young man, grabbing his arms as he stood up, and I slammed my forehead into his nose. The crunch of bones breaking under the impact drew a laugh from my throat.

Billy collapsed at my feet and I shifted, moving back a few steps before slamming the side of one hand into the soft tissue where his neck joined his shoulder. He cried out in pain and tried to crawl away. I threw back my head and roared. A punch to his temple was followed by a kick to his side, right under the ribs.

The young man sprawled on the ground, holding one hand pressed to his side where I'd kicked him. He held out the other hand in a feeble attempt to block my attacks. I stepped back, savoring his pain, taking my time.

The door to the shed opened, and the older man stepped through. My eyes went to him, my night vision showing me the shotgun he held. His eyes darted around, searching for me. I crouched down, keeping my breathing shallow and controlled. Billy's pants and moans covered the little noise I made.

The older man held up the gun, jerking it around at every sound he thought he heard, as he made his way over to the injured young man. I smiled. This was going to be easy.

He turned to check on Billy, reaching one hand out to feel for injuries. I gathered my feet under me, ignoring the strain on my weakened muscles. I launched myself into the air with barely a rustle of my shoes leaving the dirty floor.

The man realized his danger too late. He tried to bring the gun up, but I landed on him before he could get a grip on it. My body slammed into him, knees first, and I wrenched the shotgun out of his hands, slapping it away with enough force to send it flying several feet.

I drove the heel of my hand into the older man's face, missing his nose and slamming it into the side of his mouth instead. I felt the pop of the jaw dislocating, and I swung the side of my other hand at his neck. He brought up his hands to clutch at his face, which blocked the deadly blow to his neck.

He fell onto the ground beside Billy, crying out for his god to save him. I adjusted my stance, standing back from them enough that they wouldn't be able to surprise me with a kick. I rolled my shoulders, taking pleasure in the ache of the stretching muscles.

A light appeared in the door, I backed away from the men on the ground, crouching down to be ready for an attack while my eyes adjusted.

"Nicola?"

Joseph pointed the flashlight at the men and out of my eyes. I could see the worry on his face as he looked at me with the indirect light. I followed the light down to the two men, cringing on the floor. I glanced down at myself, noting that my shirt was still pushed up around my armpits, and my pants were unbuttoned.

I laughed, letting the anger fade away. My laugh turned slightly hysterical before I brought it under control.

"Are you okay?" Joseph asked. "Am I too late?"

"I'm fine," I said. "And you are just in time to stop me from killing them." Another giggle escaped my throat as I limped past the two men and walked out of the shed into the cool night air.

CHAPT 19

Joseph found a nearby campground that had a shower and laundry area. I took the hottest shower I could manage while he ran a load of laundry for us. After I shampooed my hair three times, I decided it was time to face what had happened.

I put on a pair of sweatpants and a sweatshirt against the chill night air and gladly accepted the hot tea that Joseph handed me. I stared into the fire while he quickly folded up the laundry and packed it away.

I knew I had to tell him what happened, and I knew I needed to tell him what I needed to do to break through my emotional hang-ups. I sighed.

"What's up?" he asked.

"I have to tell you," I said. "I just really wish we could skip the telling and the admitting, and the inevitable crying."

Joseph nodded. "I totally understand. They are just words, but that doesn't change that some words are almost too damn hard to say."

I nodded and sipped my tea. "True fact."

"So, I take it you didn't run off at the first sign of a lead when I wasn't looking then?" Joseph asked.

I glanced at him and smiled. He was giving me an easy start. "Nope," I said. "Did the ravens find you?"

"Yeah. I was only about an hour or so away, you know."

I frowned. "Why so close?"

He shook his head. "I had this weird dream just after you disappeared," he admitted. "It bugged me, and I couldn't shake the feeling that it was important. But I didn't know what it meant, so I just stayed where I was."

I chuckled. "It meant I suck at dream walking, and you have some crazy snakes in your head." I laughed at Joseph's expression. After a moment, he shook his head and laughed with me.

"You tried to dream walk me to call for help," he said. "Wow, the things we end up doing."

I nodded. "Yeah." I sipped my tea again.

Joseph waited, letting me set the pace for the next step.

"The young one tried to rape me," I said, in a rush. "Apparently, daddy never let him get married, and he was sexually frustrated, so he thought he could just go ahead and 'marry' me."

Joseph whistled. "How do you find all these guys who think that a marriage license falls from the sky when you get laid?"

I shrugged. "Mad skills?"

He snorted. "Well, then, I'm not gonna give you any crap about beating the shit out of the two of them," he said. "They very much deserved what you gave them and more."

I sighed. "Yeah, well, it almost didn't happen," I admitted. I caught his questioning look. "I was terrified. I locked up. I froze. I could barely manage a feeble resistance. Then..."

Joseph waited for me to continue. "Then?" he prompted after a long moment.

I shook my head. "I don't know how to explain it."

"Just try."

"It's like, I could hear her," I said. "My inner monster. My inner victim. I could hear her screaming because I had promised it would never happen again." I choked on a sob. "I was supposed to be strong enough that it would never happen again."

Joseph reached over and laid his hand on my shoulder. "I know," he said. "We make promises to ourselves. And sometimes, we just don't keep them."

I nodded. "It was feeling her pain at being betrayed," I said. "No, it was feeling MY pain at my own failure. That's what let me Berserk."

Joseph cocked his head to the side. "So you were Berserking," he said. "I thought you were, but then you just stopped. I wasn't sure if you'd gotten more control or if I was just jumping to conclusions."

I shook my head. "It was weird," I admitted. "It was like I'd made a decision and that allowed me to have more influence over the Berserker. I could see in the dark, and I was able to let the 11th Runespell guide my fighting. Before, when I took out Zaro, I fought the influence of the Runespell when I was Berserking."

Joseph nodded. "That sounds like progress."

"Yeah, but I have more work to do," I admitted. "I'm going to have to do more shadow work with these traumas."

"But not this day," Joseph said. "This day, you are going to sleep, then we are going to catch up to this Stella Kormer."

I snorted. "We are two days more behind than we were before," I pointed out.

Joseph nodded. "Yeah, but I spent a day sitting on my ass with two bars of internet," he said, waggling his eyebrows. "And I found a place about 70 miles north that has caves like the one you found in the astral plane."

I perked up. "Seriously?"

"Yeah, there's some warnings posted about it being dangerous to spelunk there," he grinned. "Plus, there's postings of local legends about a Grimm living in those caves."

"A Grimm? Like the big black dog that foretells death?"

"Yup. I figure, if we are this far behind anyways, it's worth the risk to catch a ride-share up that way."

I nodded. "You rock so hard." I yawned through the words.

"Get some sleep," he said. "I'll have a pick up scheduled before breakfast is over in the morning."

CHAPT 20

I stepped into the astral plane. I looked around and took a deep breath. There were no Fears showing up this time, probably because I was too tired to be nervous of getting sucked into astral addiction again. I was here for a reason.

"I thought you might try this."

I turned sheepishly and waved at Joseph. "Hey, I thought you were asleep."

"Ditto," he said. "But I also knew you've been so focused on this quest, you might do something stupid, like astral travel instead of getting much-needed sleep."

I shrugged. "What can I say?" I said. "I'm predictable."

He shook his head. "What are you looking for, Nicola?"

I sighed. "It's about what Fenrir said," I admitted. "That Stella isn't the one who is going to release him."

"You think you can find out who it is?" Joseph asked. "How?"

I grinned. "I'm gonna piss off a god and hope he slips," I said. "Wanna come?"

Joseph shook his head. "I can't leave you alone for anything."

He took my hands and we closed our eyes. I pulled us with the world-tilting lurch into Jehovah's garden. I dropped Joseph's hands and walked along the slate-stone path.

"Come on," I said. "It doesn't get less pretty if you don't gawk at it."

Joseph snorted in response and jogged to catch up to me. "So, where is God?" he asked.

"I don't know," I said. I raised my voice to a yell. "Hiding because he's afraid of me?"

A sensual chuckle came from behind us, and we turned to find Satan standing there. He was wearing his sexy suit and looking suave as usual.

"Nicola, my love!" he drawled. "What gift have you brought me?"

"Down boy!" I snapped. I shot a glance at Joseph. "This is Lucy. Lucy, Joseph."

"Don't mind her," Satan said to Joseph, stepping forward and holding out his hand. Joseph reflexively took it, and the embodiment of evil lifted it to his mouth and kissed Joseph's hand. "She's just jealous of me."

Joseph swallowed and glanced at me, pulling his hand away from the devilishly handsome man. "Is he always so... aggressive?" he asked me.

"Yeah," I said. "Lucy thinks he can get what he wants with sex appeal."

"Hmm," Joseph said, turning back to Satan. "Maybe you need a little more practice at being subtle," he suggested.

Satan's face dropped into a scowl, and I burst out laughing.

"I can see why the two of you get along," the devil sneered. "Why are you here?"

I pushed my laughter down to barely controlled giggles. "I just thought I'd let you know that your rednecks are down for the count," I gasped between chuckles. "And I was wondering if you have anyone on your side who isn't a crazy loser."

Satan frowned. "The grocery owner failed me, then." He nodded. "It was expected. You were still delayed."

I grinned.

"Not as much as you would think," Joseph said.

Satan shot a glare at him, then glanced at me.

"We have an ace in the hole," I assured him in a stage whisper.

Satan shrugged. "No matter," he said. "You may get there, but you won't be able to stop both of them once they are there."

I nodded. "I've defeated every single one of your guys," I pointed out. "What makes this one any different?"

Satan grinned. "Oh, dear sweet Nicola," he crooned. "You keep forgetting that you haven't actually defeated them all."

I frowned as he leaned forward, putting his face very close to mine.

"You keep letting one of them get away, don't you?" he murmured. He straightened. "Don't act like you are some kind of undefeated champion of good and right. You've been taken down. And you've missed, more than once. It will happen again."

I laughed. "It's only a matter of time before I get all your little minions," I said. "Now stop playing around. We want to talk to Jehovah."

Satan rolled his eyes. "Oh, right, and I'm just going to do what you want of me."

I smirked and turned to Joseph. "I told you Jehovah was too chicken to face me."

Satan opened his mouth to retort, and I bawked at him, clucking like a chicken. The more he scowled, the louder I clucked. Joseph clapped his hands over his mouth, trying not to laugh at the King of Hell.

Finally, he crossed his hands over his chest and disappeared.

Joseph glanced around. "Well, that wasn't very productive."

I smiled. "Just wait," I said. "I think he's still trying to convince me I was wrong when I saw Satan and Jehovah as the same being."

"I assure you," a deep voice intoned behind us. "You were wrong."

We turned to find Jehovah standing there, his hands tucked into the sleeves of his cream robes, his long white beard hanging over them like a waterfall.

"See?" I said to Joseph cheerfully.

Joseph frowned at the god. "You look familiar."

"Yeah," I said. "He looks like Satan, because they are the same person."

Jehovah scowled.

Joseph shook his head. "No," he murmured. "I mean, you're right, but that's not who he is reminding me of."

I turned to Jehovah. "Let's see, you are pretending you aren't Satan, so let's catch you up. I took out your redneck goons, I'm going to catch Stella, and whoever else you send is as good as defeated. So there."

Joseph held up his hand, closing one eye while staring at the god. He looked like he was playing that game where you cover someone's face with your thumb.

Jehovah stared at me without expression. "Good for you," he said after a moment.

I frowned. "Wait, no," I said. "I mean, yes, good for me, but you shouldn't be saying that."

"I've got it!" Joseph yelled. "You look a bit like that guy from the mall."

"Who?" I said.

Joseph turned to me. "You remember, outside of Keith's little exhibit. That guy who came up to you." He snapped his fingers. "Mr. Covis..."

"Corvus," I said, turning to stare at Jehovah. Now that Joseph had mentioned it, I could see some similarities in the eyes and mouth. "Except that was really Odin."

"You dare!" Jehovah roared. "Never compare me to that despicable creature! I am God, not he! I am worshipped the world over, not he!"

The god grew, his eyes flashing with actual lightning. I grabbed Joseph's hands.

"Time to go!" I told him.

"I conquered death itself, not he! I rule the Western world, not he! I will have my apocalypse! Mine! Not his! Not hi—"

I pulled us back into the astral plane, cutting off Jehovah's rant. We dropped our hands, both of us panting as the adrenaline that had flooded into our systems in fear began to drain out again.

"Holy crap-cicles!" I said.

"What was that?" Joseph asked.

I shook my head. "Not a clue. The only other time he's done that was when I found out he was Satan." I frowned. "He does seem to be rather sensitive about being compared to other gods and the like."

Joseph nodded. "Well, that was... fun, but I don't think we learned much from it."

"Nope," I agreed. "Time to catch some Z's." I waved to him. "See you in the morning."

Joseph nodded, and I stepped back into my body, quickly falling asleep.

CHAPT 21

I chewed on my lip while we sped down the highway. I was worried, and I didn't know how to explain it so that it wasn't just me worrying out loud. I hated that I couldn't just share things like that. I had to have a reason for saying the words, whether it be to get advice or warn someone of what might happen.

I glanced over at Joseph. It wasn't his fault I felt this way, but I could still feel the irritation building that he didn't just know. If he knew, I wouldn't have to say it. Maybe he could find a way to relieve my worries. It was unlikely though.

I was worried about what I could only imagine was an impending conflict. Would I be able to make the right decisions? Would I be able to pull up the Berserker if I needed to? Would I figure out who Stella would give the Runespells to before they could free Fenrir?

What if I was too late? What if I found myself in some kind of fight with the monstrous wolf?

I swallowed. I wasn't sure I'd be able to handle that. And I couldn't think of anything that Joseph could do to help. But then, maybe I was ignoring my party like he'd said before.

I took a deep breath and looked over at him again. This time, I caught his attention and he smiled.

"You look nervous," he said.

I nodded.

He reached over and patted my hand. "You can do this, Nicola. I'm sure of it."

I grimaced. "What about your doubts and fears?"

He shrugged. "I guess I've realized that they have more to do with me than they do with you."

"Except they were about me."

"Yeah, but not entirely." He gave me a crooked smile. "I think I was more afraid because I didn't really understand. It wasn't that I don't trust you, it was that I felt out of control of all of it."

"So what changed?" I asked.

"Nothing except my perspective. If I trust you, I have to trust you even when I can't do anything about what or how you do things."

I grabbed his hand and squeezed. "Thanks. That helps."

The car pulled into a lot, and we thanked the driver when he popped the trunk so we could get our packs. We snapped the buckles in place without a word and headed back among the trees.

•   •   •

I scowled up at the sun, mostly hidden by the trees, just past its apex. It was surprisingly hot despite the shade of thousands of leaves. I reached for my canteen and took a swig.

"Are we there yet?" I called to Joseph.

He shot a dirty look over his shoulder. "Pretty much," he said. "We will have to do some exploring to find the right cave, but we are in the right area."

"So you don't know exactly where to go?" I asked. Anxiety rose in my gut. "How are we going to find it in time?"

Joseph shrugged. "Look, it's not like we have GPS coordinates or anything," he pointed out. "I'm doing what I can with the information we have."

I stared at him for a moment, then nodded. "I know, I'm just getting tense about the whole thing."

He offered me a smile and pointed to a faint trail heading into the trees. "We can check this one, first."

I grimaced. It wasn't the best solution, fumbling around in the underbrush to search for the right place, but I couldn't think of any other options.

We headed down the trail, watching the ground carefully so we didn't lose it. Sweat dripped down my neck and back, soaking into my cotton shirt. I wiped a strand of hair from my eyes where it had come free of its braid and peered ahead for some sign of the giant tree.

After several minutes of struggling through ferns and scraggly bushes, Joseph stopped. "I don't think we are going to find it this way," he said. "Let's head back to the main trail."

I nodded and turned on my heel, my eyes scanning the brush for the path we'd just come down. It only took us a few minutes to get back to the trail, but I could tell that Joseph was just as disappointed as I was.

"We should grab some food," he said. "It's been hours since we stopped for lunch."

I slipped the pack off my shoulders and dug in one of the pockets for a granola bar. "Eat as we walk," I said. "We have to get there as soon as possible."

Joseph nodded, hefting his own pack back onto his shoulders and clipping it before unwrapping his granola bar and stuffing the wrapper into his pocket.

I let my legs find their stride, keeping up with Joseph's longer limbs. We ate our granola in silence, sipping at our canteens to wash the dry snack down. The food hit my stomach, and I could feel the energy coming back into my legs.

After this, I was going to be in the best shape I'd ever been. I'd always enjoyed walking, but hiking was another level of exercise. I distracted myself from my frustration by visualizing the strength building in my thighs and calves. I adjusted my pack and tested my arm muscles against the weight of the bag.

"Oh man!" Joseph exclaimed. "Whew!"

I opened my mouth to ask what was going on and the scent hit me. The skunk musk was faint but potent, and I wrinkled my nose in reaction to it. I picked up my pace, noting that Joseph did the same. The scent would linger no matter what, but it would be better to get through it quickly.

I glanced around as we hurried along the path, wondering if the skunk was still close by. It wasn't likely, but I didn't want to be surprised by the creature appearing suddenly and taking exception to our presence with another spritz of au de skunk.

I smiled to myself at the visual of a skunk chattering at us for some slight. I tried to remember what kind of skunks lived in the area, but I kept seeing a spotted skunk in my mind's eye.

The spotted skunk from the astral plane, in fact.

I gasped and stumbled to a halt. "Odin's Left Eye, I'm so stupid sometimes!"

Joseph stopped and turned to look at me.

"Skunk!" I said. "The skunk led me to the tree in the astral plane."

He nodded slowly. "Okay, but how are you going to follow a smell?" he asked. "It's not like you're a dog and can sniff it out."

I remembered when I had followed Joseph's scent after my run-in with the cougar, and I smiled. "Nope," I said. "I'm a cat person." I tugged at the memory, feeding it with the feeling of a predator's satisfaction. My vision washed yellow, and a pale brown mist appeared, floating across the trail.

I followed it with my eyes, noting that it became less faded ahead of us. I growled and stalked the scent, trusting that Joseph would follow. After a few yards, the scent turned off the trail, tracing a barely visible deer path. I pushed through the brush, barely conscious of how I was twisting my body to minimize the noise. Joseph crashed through with a lot more cracking and snapping of branches.

The path twisted down a steep hill, curving around boulders and large trees as it went. I stepped lightly, noticing roots that might trip, vines that might snag my clothing. I smiled when Joseph cursed behind me, obviously not doing as well navigating the trail.

The path rounded a large mound of moss-covered boulders and spilled out into a small clearing. My eyes immediately went to the side of the hill, following the exposed roots up to the tree that towered above the rest, stretching over the clearing like a giant awning.

I heard Joseph come up behind me, the green of his scent drifting on the breeze into my line of sight. He inhaled sharply and stopped just behind my left shoulder.

"Holy gods," he breathed. "Is that what you saw?"

I snorted. "Of course not," I murmured. "What I saw was much more impressive, but this is the physical world. It's pretty much the same thing."

I could almost feel Joseph rolling his eyes at me as he brushed past.

"It looks like we got here first," he said. He peered at the opening just barely visible under the hanging roots of the tree. "You ready to go spelunking?"

I looked at the cave. The memory of Fenrir washed over me like ice water, flushing the yellow from my sight. I shook my head and crossed my arms over my chest to hold back the shudder.

"No," I said. "We might get lost in the tunnels. Better to just rest and get ready for whoever shows up."

Joseph turned to look at me. His expression was thoughtful, but he nodded in agreement. "If we go over here, we can set up a small camp without being seen by anyone coming down that path."

"Okay," I said, shrugging off the pack. "I'm going to look around some more. Just to check that no one is on our heels."

I dropped my pack next to his and walked away. I could tell he knew I was getting scared again, but I wasn't ready to hear empty reassurances. All he could tell me was that I could do it, but I simply couldn't believe it.

The only thing I knew for certain was that I didn't have a choice in the matter.

Chapt 22

Joseph finally talked me into sitting down for a while. The exhaustion of the last few days combined with the warm sunlight sifting through the leaves, and I slumped over within a few minutes, dozing. A snapping branch jerked me awake, and I squinted into the setting sun. A dark outline appeared against the sunlight, sending me scrambling for my feet.

"Calm down, Nicola," Joseph said. "It's just me."

I dropped back down into my seat, taking a deep breath to calm the adrenaline reaction. He moved out of the line of the sun, and I could see him clearly, his arms filled with dry sticks. Dead leaves stuck out of his jacket pocket. He would use that to start a fire quickly.

"How long was I out?" I asked.

He shrugged. "A few hours, I guess. Not that you missed anything." He turned to look out at the forested space surrounding us. "I doubt there's a single person for miles."

I sighed. "There only needs to be one," I pointed out. "And I doubt we would be able to tell they were out there until it was too late."

"I suppose you're right," he said, dropping the dry sticks in a pile against the steep slope of a boulder at the base of the hill a few feet from where I sat, my back against another smaller boulder.

I shifted my shoulders, enjoying the warmth of the rock against my back. I knew I should get up and keep watch, but I was comfortable, so I stared at Joseph as he made up a small fire pit and began snapping sticks and placing them in a cone around the dried leaves and vines. His movements were practiced and methodical, and it gave me a feeling of routine and comfort. It seemed that, so long as Joseph built the fire, nothing could go wrong in the world. Within a few minutes, the fire was catching on the sticks, crackling as he fed larger pieces into it.

He looked up and smiled at me. "There," he said, affecting a British accent. "Give us a bit, and it'll be time for tea."

I chuckled and rolled my eyes. A flicker of movement caught my attention in the growing shadows of the forest. I focused on the movement, trying to make sense of it. The shadows coalesced into a humanoid shape running across the clearing. I yelled and scrambled to my feet.

Joseph jumped up and spun around, meeting the attacker head on. I straightened up in time to see Joseph grappling with a woman. She screeched in his face, and he held her wrists while she tried to claw and kick at him.

"Stella!" I yelled. "Stop it!"

I called up the Berserker, letting the yellow wash over my vision. The shadows immediately sprang into sharp focus as my pupils changed. The song of protection fell from my lips while the pendant burned against my skin.

I waited a moment for an opening, then pressed in close against her back. I wrapped my arms under Stella's, reaching up and locking my hands behind her head. She struggled against my hold, her arms splayed out like a scarecrow.

Stella screamed like a banshee and dropped to her knees. The change in position let her slip out of my hold. I lunged after her, grabbing for her arms. She rolled onto her back with her knees up to her chest, and I backed off before she could kick out at me.

Her eyes narrowed as she realized we were at a stand-off. If she changed position, I would be able to move in on her. As long as she had her legs ready to lash out, I had to keep my distance, but she was stuck on her back.

I smiled. A stand-off was fine by me. I just had to keep her and the mystery person from going into the cave. I didn't need to win any fights to do that.

Joseph came up beside me and stared down at her. "Is that it?" he asked. "Did we win?"

I shrugged, watching the woman on the ground. He turned to her, looking her over. I noticed her shudder when his eyes moved across her body. Joseph noticed, too, and he crouched down beside her.

"Someone's hurt you," he said softly. "Is that why you are doing this?"

"What do you care?" she growled.

Joseph shrugged. "I care."

"Ha!" she spat. "No man has ever cared 'cept to tell me what to cook and how he wanted to get off."

Stella cringed. It seemed she realized how much she had given away with that comment. Joseph just squatted beside her and watched her.

Stella's eyes darted from him to me and back. After a moment, she grew visibly uncomfortable under his gaze. "What makes you different?"

Joseph sucked his teeth. "Well, I don't know. Except I cook just fine on my own, and I have no desire for you to get me off."

She shot him a dirty look. "Think you're too good for me, huh?"

Joseph laughed. "No, no. Just too gay for you."

Stella looked confused for a moment. "Never pegged you for a sodomite."

He shrugged off the comment. "Who hurt you, Stella? Why would you do this?"

The woman scowled. "You don't understand," she muttered. "You can't just ignore a call."

My eyes narrowed, and I glanced at Joseph. His expression tightened.

"A call, huh?" he said. "You mean like a calling, like from God."

She glanced at me and back to Joseph again. "Yeah. You can make fun if you want, but it's real."

Joseph nodded. "I know it's real," he admitted.

Stella looked surprised. "I did just what He said," she whispered. "He came to me and told me what to do."

"Where did you get the pendant?" I growled. "How did you get it?"

She frowned. "They came in the mail," she said. "Guard took a bribe to let jewelry in, I guess. I was gonna throw them away until I got a new cellmate."

"Nancy," I snarled.

Stella gave me a disgusted look. "Yeah, Nancy," she snapped. "First person to ever do anything for me."

"She protected you," Joseph guessed.

The woman nodded. "She helped me understand what God asked me to do."

"And what did he ask you to do, exactly?" he asked.

Stella frowned, pressing her lips together. "Don't you know?" she asked. "Isn't that why you're trying to stop me?"

I barked out a laugh. "We know what we were told," I snarled.

"Just like you," Joseph pointed out. "We prefer to make our own choices with all the information if we can."

Stella shrugged. "I was told how to get away from the guards," she said, reluctantly. "I was told there was someone here who was being held prisoner - no trial, no crime, no escape. These pendants are miracles for people like me and him."

I laughed. "Well, that's mostly the truth," I said, injecting a note of cruelty in my words. "Too bad it misses the whole damn point."

Joseph frowned at me. "Nicola, that's not fair."

"Don't talk to me about fair," I snapped. "She's about to unleash a monster on the world, one who can't wait to begin the bloodbath he didn't have the chance to bring before." I turned on Stella. "Charles Manson didn't commit any crimes either. You gonna tell me he's innocent, too?"

The woman glared at me.

Joseph stood up, facing me. "Nicola," he warned. "This woman was manipulated—"

"Of course she was," I cried. "We all are! Every one of us is a puppet on some god's strings, and we are all just trying to do the best we can." I stepped forward, nearly nose to nose with him, glaring up into his face. "So fucking what. It doesn't make what she's trying to do less of a disaster."

Joseph stared down at me, disappointment and anger filling his expression. "You could try showing her a little empathy," he murmured. "She's more like you than you think."

"No," I snapped. "I am perfectly aware of how much we are alike. What's bugging you, Saint Joseph, is that I don't care."

I ignored the shock that spread over his face. I glanced down at Stella only to find that she had taken advantage of our argument to scoot away and get to her feet. She took off into the darkness that had fallen during our exchange.

I roared at her and shoved Joseph aside before launching myself at her. In my anger, I overshot the mark and landed in front of her. I spun around and grasped at her as she ducked down and slid to a stop before running back the other way.

Joseph stepped in front of her and caught her in his long arms. He locked one hand around his other wrist, squeezing enough to hold her firmly with her arms pinned to her sides. She threw back her head and screamed, kicking with her feet.

I stalked up to them and glared at them both. The yellow wash of night-vision still gave me an advantage in the firelight, but I was feeling the frustration of not giving my rage a physical outlet.

Somewhere in the underbrush, a loud pop sounded out. It seemed familiar, like I should know the sound. Before my conscious mind could process it, the sigil burned on my skin, and I dropped and rolled to avoid the gunfire.

My mind clouded over as the memories of two years before came back. Popping noises had filled the small apartment while Joseph, Mercy and I ran for cover dragging Keith along with us. He had died, slowly and painfully, turning what we thought we'd known on its head and giving us the Runespells with his last breath.

I struggled to hold on to the Berserker, trying to turn my fear and pain into anger, but it slipped away. I crouched by the rocky hillside, panting, with my eyes blurring with tears.

The memory of Keith's death brought more memories roaring to the surface. I saw Mercy turning away from me as a hidden door closed, sacrificing herself so that Joseph and I could get away from the demons that were intent on stopping us. Bob's angry expression floated behind my closed eyelids as I remembered the feel of monstrous claws holding my arms too tightly.

The claws turned into fabric straps and the many hands of the Brothers and Sisters of the Center. Bob's face wavered as if I saw it underwater, the ice water washing me into the astral plane where Fears waited to tear me apart. The claws covering my mouth to keep me from screaming morphed into Nancy's firm hold over my mouth and nose. Her voice rang in my ears, cold and controlled, to shut up and do what I was told. Panic flooded through me, and the Fears howled with glee as the ripped into my astral flesh.

I was ripped out of the astral by the defibrillators, and I landed in Jehovah's garden. I saw the flashing smile of Satan transform into Zaro's grin as he watched my resistance crumble under his touch. His rough, uncaring hands became Billy's fumbling grasp, roaming over my body as if it was some plaything to use without concern for my feelings. I felt them all over my skin, touching and taking, consuming my will and drinking in my pain.

Their voices merged, chanting "Nicola, Nicola" as if they loved me. The rhythmic chant felt physical, like a bass thrumming into my gut. Bob's face, scarred from the burns I'd given him years before, floated before my eyes, his lips pulled tight in a grotesque grimace in the flickering firelight. I screamed until my voice ripped at my throat.

CHAPT 23

My breath escaped in whimpers while I struggled to force the flood of images from my mind. I closed my eyes and focused on my heartbeat, letting the rhythm sooth me as it gradually slowed. After several long minutes, the memories stopped drowning me, and I opened my eyes.

The fire was low, a glow fluttering in the darkness. I saw Joseph lying near it, and I tried to force my muscles into moving. I crawled unsteadily across the clearing to his side. He was very still, his breathing shallow. I laid my hand on his arm and shook him gently. His eyes fluttered but didn't open. A dark spot on his shirt gleamed in the dim light. I touched it, and my fingers came back red.

"Joseph!" I croaked, my voice still rough from screaming. "Joseph, you can't die on me!"

This time, his eyes opened. He looked around, confused and unfocused, before his gaze locked on my face. "Nicola," he whispered.

"What happened?" I asked.

"Gunshots."

I nodded. "I remember that part."

"Stella... bullets all missed her," he murmured. "Like... magic."

I frowned. "Are you sure?"

He nodded, and I sat back. There was a Runespell that protected the holder from arrows. It wouldn't be too much of a stretch if it actually protected the wielder from missile weapons of all kinds.

I suddenly realized that Stella had said "they" had come to her in the mail. She'd been talking about more than one pendant, and I'd missed it.

"Dammit," I growled. "Where did she go? Did you see who was shooting?"

Joseph coughed. "In the cave..." he whispered.

I pulled out my phone, checking it for a signal. "I'm going to have to go up to the main trail to call for help," I said. "Can you hold on until I get back?"

"No," Joseph said, forcing the words out. "You have to stop them—"

"No, I can't leave you like this." I shook my head. "I can't risk losing you."

He grabbed my arm. "It was Bob," he ground out. "They went into the cave."

My eyes went wide, and I choked back a gasp. "Bob? He was really here?"

Joseph pulled on my arm. "I get it, Nicola," he said. "Took me too long, but I get it. You can't put your wants before your duty."

"That's not what this—"

"If I am going to die," he said, swallowing hard, "you have to let me. You have to stop them first. You have to go after them now."

Tears filled my eyes. "No," I moaned. "I have to get you help."

Joseph huffed a weak laugh. "Helping me won't do any good," he wheezed. "Not if they free Fenrir. Not if they get the end of the world they've been after."

He grabbed my phone. "I'll hold on to this... until you get back."

I felt my lower lip trembling. "I don't want to," I cried. "I don't know if I can face him."

Joseph grabbed my hand and squeezed it with his. "You will," he whispered. "You have to. It's not the right choice. But it's the only choice."

I shook my head, tears dripping down my cheeks. I opened my mouth, ready to protest again.

"If you don't do this," Joseph growled weakly, "you will be murdering Ella... and Maria... and me." He glared at me, panting to get the words out. "Grow up, Nicola. Take back your power... and kick their asses."

A sob burst out of my raw throat, but I knew he was right. I hated him for being right, and I hated every person who had helped me along my path for bringing me to this moment. But he was right.

I pushed myself to my feet and slapped the tears from my face. I didn't look back at Joseph as I stumbled towards the cave. If I looked back, I knew I would break down again.

I staggered into the hanging roots, pushing at them belatedly. They dragged across my face, scratching at my cheeks. It took another ten steps before the weak light from the fire and the stars was completely gone, and I stood in the darkness.

I tried to bring up the Berserker, but the fear kept creeping in and washing away the power. I took a shaky breath and clenched my hands into fists.

"Come on," I muttered. "Joseph was right. Time to get it done. There's no other choice. This is life or death, right now, and not just mine. People are counting on me, and there's no one to pick up the ball if I drop it."

I shut my eyes tightly and pulled up memories of hanging out with Joseph, Ella, and Maria running in the yard. I saw Hound Dog's grin, Ames' scowling face, Huginn and Muninn flapping their wings happily.

I remembered Mercy, staring at me in shock, then dropping to one knee in front of me. She had just learned the full extent of what had happened at the Center, and what I'd begun to recover from. She had given me the highest honor from one warrior to another, a salute of impossible odds overcome.

I lifted my chin. I had gone through some major crap. It had broken me, more than once. But I kept getting up and moving forward. That was the best I could do, and it was what I needed to do. Each time my experiences kicked me in the gut, sending me to my knees, I would catch my breath, get up, and take a step forward.

I took a deep breath and stepped forward, pulling at the strength inside me. I didn't try for the feeling of being stronger than anyone else. I didn't try for the feeling of being a warrior. Those things weren't what made me truly strong.

I grasped at the grim determination I'd felt when facing Zaro. I reached for the anger and frustration of not being able to fix things, and the hollow satisfaction of being able to avenge myself and others. I pulled up the harsh justice of evil people being stopped, but only temporarily. And I embraced the wretched and painful love I felt for myself and others who had endured the same kind of victimization.

The power flowed through me, an acrid and bitter taste in the back of my throat. I was broken. I had been broken, and I would be broken again. But I didn't have to let that stop me, even if the fear clogged my throat. Even if the pain drove me to weeping again and again. Each day I kept going was a victory over those who would see me fail.

Yellow-green night vision washed over my sight, and I could see a blend of orange and red scent-energy trails. They were from Stella and Bob. I took one step, then another. My feet moved faster until I was nearly jogging through the narrow tunnels.

I ducked under roots hanging down over my head like beams in a half-constructed house. I twisted my hips to get around tight spots where boulders jutted into the space. My breath huffed rhythmically, echoing over and over to harmonize with itself.

Something grabbed my foot and sent me sprawling against a boulder pushing into my path. I glanced back to see a large root, at least an inch in diameter, arching up from the ground like a miniature bridge across the path.

"Death by deciduous," I muttered. "What a way to go."

I straightened up and kept walking, my footsteps a little more cautious this time. I tried to watch where I put my feet while following the scent trail. It wasn't as easy as it seemed. Several times, the trail branched off where Stella and Bob had found a dead end and backtracked. If I chose the wrong direction, I wasted time following it into a tunnel and right back out again.

It was getting harder to see, even with my night vision. As the minutes passed, I felt the pressure to catch up to them, and I found myself jogging through the narrow tunnels again.

Once more, I tripped on an exposed root or rock sticking up from the ground. I caught myself on the wall where it curved in front of me. A sharp pain lanced through my hand, and I glanced down to see dark blood on my palm. I remembered my trip through the caves in the astral plane. Twice tripping, cutting my hand the second time.

I blew out my breath. Sometimes those experiences were metaphors, sometimes they were predictions. There was no user's manual to tell which was which. But it reminded me that I'd been in these caves before.

The next time the scent trail branched off, I peered in each direction, looking for a familiar landmark. I noticed an oddly shaped root hanging down from the ceiling in one direction. It seemed familiar, so I headed that way. After a moment, I smiled. It looked like I'd chosen the right direction.

I realized there was a light shining ahead. The rocks were easier to see in the darkness, and I moved with more confidence. I could see a bend in the tunnel ahead of me, and I slowed down to peer around it before I gave myself away.

As I glanced around the edge of the rock that formed the inner curve of the wall, a familiar voice echoed through the tunnel, letting me know that I had found them. My stomach roiled.

CHAPT 24

"Just give me the Runespells," Bob snarled. "That's all that is left of your mission."

"Why should I trust you? You shot me!"

Stella sounded more petulant than angry. I swallowed my emotional reaction and peeked around the rock wall. She was walking a step ahead of Bob, holding a phone with the flashlight activated. The bright light shone blindingly in the darkness, but it was pointed away from me.

Bob held his hands clenched into fists at his side, one fist curled around a handgun. He stalked after the woman with every movement tense.

"You have the pendant that protects you from being shot," he bit out. "I knew you would be safe. I was shooting for those two pains in the ass outside."

"That's not the point," Stella said. "I'm so tired of men telling me what to do. You'll get these things when you need to use them, but I don't have to hand them over yet."

Bob grabbed Stella's arm. "You had better not be thinking of keeping them for yourself," he said, his voice filled with warning. "You were chosen to be a courier, nothing more."

The woman stared at him, her eyes wide and her expression frozen. Her shoulders were hunched and tense. Her hands made loose fists, palm-side out in front of her torso. Her gaze dropped to the gun in Bob's other hand. She turned her head, looking up at Bob slightly sideways.

I recognized the look on her face and the way she held her body. She was waiting for an indication of what he would do. It was the look of a beaten dog being approached by a stranger, full of fear but unsure of whether to fight or cower. I would lay money down that Stella had been abused in one form or another for most of her life.

"You're right," Stella murmured, a tone of deference lacing through her voice. "I'm just supposed to deliver these pendants."

Bob released her arm, his expression relaxing. He held up his hand, palm up.

Stella shook her head. "I'm supposed to deliver them to the wolf," she said, emphasizing the last word. "I'm supposed to give them to the one who shows up to free him."

Bob rolled his eyes. "Stupid woman," he growled, ignoring the way the woman flinched at the sharp tone in his voice. "That's me! I'm showing up to free the wolf."

Stella pursed her lips. "Probably," she admitted. "But I'd rather do what I was told, just like I was told. That way, I won't get it wrong." She turned and started walking forward again. She was trying to be casual about it, but her shoulders were still tense and pulled up. She called to Bob over her shoulder, "If you show up, you get the jewelry."

Bob stalked after her, and I followed, staying out of sight and watching for an opportunity that wouldn't get me shot. I clutched the pendants at my neck unconsciously, whispering the protection song as the Eleventh Runespell grew hot against my chest.

I rounded another corner and pulled back when I saw that Bob and Stella had only made it a few feet ahead of me. I ducked down into the shadows and watched them. Bob had grabbed Stella by both arms this time and was pushing her against the wall to the tunnels.

"You don't get to make the rules," Bob growled. "We are on the same side. Why are you so desperate to keep the pendants?"

Stella swallowed, her eyes huge in her thin face. "Why are you so desperate to get them?" she bit out.

Bob's hold relaxed, and Stella pulled her arms free. "We have our own jobs to do," she pointed out. "Just let me do mine and stop being so mean about it."

She waited for a moment, but Bob just stood there, staring at her with narrowed eyes. Finally, she moved to walk away. Bob followed her, and I stood up, staying close behind them. I realized that Stella was the weak link.

After a few more feet, a harsh gibbering echoed faintly through the tunnel, bouncing off the rock walls. Stella jumped at the sound and stopped suddenly, dropping her hand to her side. The flashlight gleamed dimly against her leg as she gaped, staring into the tunnels ahead.

Bob nearly ran into her back and overbalanced when he stepped back. He caught himself on the wall and took a step forward, but his foot had found one of the roots looping across the narrow path. He let out a low curse as his body lurched forward.

He crashed into Stella, who was still standing frozen in place. She fell forward and the phone, with its LED flashlight still glaring in the darkness, flew out of her hand and into the tunnel ahead of her. The phone landed with the light down. As the cavern plunged into darkness, I saw the handgun clatter to the rock at Bob's feet.

I felt my eyes shift in the near-pitch blackness, and I leaped forward before my eyes had even fully adjusted to the night vision. My eyes refocused and I could see Bob's face becoming clear as I crashed into him, tucking my knees for maximum impact.

Bob let out a grunting cry when I hit him, landing in a full sprawl onto his stomach with me on his back. I let my fear feed my anger, and I grabbed the wiry man's head with both hands before he could recover. I pulled it towards me, then thrust it back, hitting his head and face against the rocky ground under us. The juicy thunk of his flesh impacting the stone sent a thrill of satisfaction down my spine.

Maybe, if I was a better person, I would have forgiven him for all he'd done to me. He'd been the one who sent the demons to kill Keith. He'd tricked me into meeting him so he could kidnap me, lock me in a basement, and threaten Joseph's life to get me to find the Runespells for him. He'd been the one to manipulate Keith into starting this whole mess to begin with.

I had broken his knee and burned him alive, and the bastard still survived. He'd gone on to bring the Gaona's into his circle. Nancy had corrupted the Healing Runespell, while Zaro had used a Runespell meant to bring comfort and safety to rape dozens of women.

Bob had told Zaro where to find my daughter. When I'd broken free of his control, he raced to my home and cut my baby's throat. I'd beaten Zaro into a coma, but not Bob. Bob had escaped again. But not this time. I slammed his face into the ground again and again until his body went limp.

A piercing light flashed in my face, and I raised my hand to block it, blinking rapidly. Stella cried out, sounding shocked. I heard a scuffling noise as the light disappeared just as suddenly as it had appeared. I shook my head to clear my vision and stood up to face the woman. She was clambering over a rock jutting up from the floor in the path, the light jerking back and forth as she moved.

I leaped forward and landed inches from where the rock broke through the packed dirt. I reached out with both hands, grabbing the woman's heavy flannel shirt. My fingertips tingled, and I bent my fingers down, claw-like. My nails scraped against the fabric, then caught on it. I pulled, jerking my whole body backward.

Stella lost her handhold and we tumbled back. I hit the ground a split second before Stella landed on me. I took the weight right on my stomach, and air whooshed out of my lungs. I grimaced with rage and twisted my body, shifting our weight so I could roll us over, exchanging our positions.

I pinned her to the ground, using my anger for strength while I gasped and panted, trying to get my breath back. Stella screeched and kicked, but I held her in place.

"Where are they?" I snarled, pushing my face close to hers. "Where are the pendants?"

She bit out several curses at me and redoubled her attempts to kick me off.

I shoved her arms above her head and held them down with one hand, digging my nails into her flesh without mercy. With my other hand, I reached down and tried to dig into her pockets. She screamed and cursed more, and her struggles made the search nearly impossible.

I grabbed her shirt and shook her until her teeth rattled. "You can tell me where they are," I spat, "or I can beat you unconscious and get them anyway."

Stella's eyes widened, and the look of fear and horror grew as she realized I was serious. "You are a monster," she whispered. "I will never help you."

I snarled. "Fine by me." I pulled my hand back, clenching it into a fist to drive into her chin.

Pain speared into my head, and I saw stars before the world went black. I blinked my eyes and managed to focus after a moment. I found myself lying on my side on the ground with a huge goose egg forming on the back of my skull.

I stared in a daze as Bob scrambled over the rock, pulling Stella behind him.

CHAPT 25

I staggered to my feet and lurched after the pair, clawing at the stone walls to pull myself up over the obstacle. I kept cursing myself for not making sure Bob was out, and cursing Bob for being his usual, undefeatable thorn in my side.

I hefted myself over the boulder and stumbled forward. The soft glow of reflected light from the phone's flashlight lead me through the tunnels after them as much as the echoing scuffles of their feet and the low murmurs of their voices.

I rounded a bend and saw them only a few feet away, standing wide-eyed and staring. The cavern was lit by two fires that burned along the length of each side of the space. They sparked with odd colors, and the wood did not darken to coal, so I decided they must be magical fires.

I already knew what Bob and Stella were staring at, so I took the opportunity and launched myself at Stella. My fingers latched onto her hair and I yanked her backwards. She fell with a cry, and Bob turned and cried out in anger. He cocked his fist to take a swing at me.

I pulled my hand free from the woman's locks and blocked his attack. I kicked out sideways, knocking Stella back to the ground before blocking another punch from Bob and attacking with a one-two punch at his chest. Bob staggered back, a hand covering his sternum.

"Give me the pendants," he yelled at Stella. "It's time to free the beast!"

I sent a kick that connected with the woman's head this time before rushing at Bob. I hit him with both fists on either side of his chest, grabbing his shirt and pushing him back into the wall. His back hit the rock with a thud. I pressed my advantage, moving my arm in front of his throat.

I heard a loud growl, like the earth itself was snarling. A clink of metal on metal echoed, and I glanced over at the wolf.

He had stepped forward, drawing the chain tight from his neck to the wall where it disappeared into the rock. His small ears were pressed flat against his head. His lips pulled back from his too-large, too-white teeth in a monstrous grimace. His long, stocky legs pushed against the ground as he strained against the chain.

He was skinny, bones sticking out from his body on all sides. The question of how, and what, he ate in the depths of this cave drifted through my mind. I tried not to consider the warnings about spelunking and the number of hikers that disappeared on the Trail each year.

I held Bob firmly against the wall as I stared at the creature before us. The firelight gave off an odd blue and yellow glow, and the beast's dark fur shone with icy white highlights. I realized the yellow night vision had faded away from my vision. I tried to pull up the Berserker again, but it slipped away.

As I dealt with my own inner struggle, the wolf-monster relaxed and settled into a sitting position. He closed his mouth and licked his chops. An odd sound rumbled in his chest.

Fenrir was laughing. "After so long," he growled. "Mortals have come to see me."

"Don't get too excited," I snapped. "We were just about to leave."

"Dear god," Stella moaned. "It talks! The beast talks!"

I rolled my eyes.

"You have come to free me?" the wolf asked. He ducked his head and gave Stella a somewhat distorted puppy-eyed expression. It might have worked if his eyes hadn't kept flashing with a demonic, reddish glint in the light.

Stella pulled herself to her feet, her wide eyes never leaving the wolf-creature. "I-I can't," she said. "He told me to bring the jewelry for someone else."

The wolf grinned. "Who told you?" He dragged out the vowels. "Who sent you?"

Stella gulped. "God," she said.

Fenrir gave a wolfish laugh, chuffing dryly. "Without a doubt," he crooned. "But which one?"

The woman shook her head. "The God," she said. "The Almighty."

The beast's ear flicked forward. "Thor?" he asked, disbelief coloring his voice.

THE CHAINS THAT BIND

Stella frowned. "Don't you know Our Lord God? The Father?"

Fenrir cocked his head to one side. "Odin? He would never send you. Maybe those stupid birds, but not you."

"He doesn't know God," Bob growled. "He's a true beast and heathen, innocent of the Word of the Lord."

Bob tried to push me off of him, but I slammed him back against the rock.

"She's talking about Jehovah," I snapped to the wolf. "Before that he was Yahweh. Before that he was a stupid desert wind god called Shaitan."

"Blasphemy!" Bob raged.

"You dare speak of God like that?" Stella cried at the same time.

The beast watched our exchanged with what could only be described as an amused expression. He lowered his head, flattening his ears in an amused expression. "Ah, Shaitan," he growled, as the echoes from the protests faded. "I recall that name. And the name before that?"

I heard humor in his voice, and I shot him a dirty look before I put my focus firmly back on keeping Bob in place. I wasn't in the mood to appreciate the beast's joke.

Fenrir laughed at my silence. "Or don't you know?" he asked. "I always wondered if any others had seen through him."

My eyes flickered back to him. "What are you talking about?"

"Shaitan," the beast purred. "Such a sad god. It was his third name, Shaitan. Always trying to one-up his brother."

"What?" I frowned. "Jehovah has a brother? Who-?"

"Shut up," Stella screamed. "Shut up, shut up! You are sinners! Blasphemers! Your words are straight from the devil himself! You cannot corrupt me! I am a true believer in the Word of God!"

I snorted. "More like Jehovah is the devil himself," I muttered with a smirk.

Bob tried to lunge forward again, snarling wordlessly at me, but I pushed him back, laughing in his face. Fenrir cocked his head, his eyes on Bob and me, then he turned back to Stella.

"Tell me, true believer," he crooned. "Why do you come to release me?"

Stella shook her head, tears streaming down her face, her wide eyes never leaving the wolf. "I-I don't," she protested. "I was to bring the pendants here. Someone else was supposed free you to do as God wills."

"Me!" Bob shouted, struggling again. "I am your savior, beast! I will free you in the name of God!"

Fenrir flicked a glance at Bob, then turned back to Stella, dismissing the man with a canine sneeze. "And why did you choose to play your part, woman?" he asked. "Why should a mortal do such a thing?"

Stella frowned, confusion flashing across her face. "Why wouldn't I do as God asked?"

Fenrir grinned. "Ah, ignorance," he said, smacking his lips. "What a friend you have been to me."

I rolled my eyes. "This monster," I said to Stella, "is going to roam the earth, killing people until the final war starts."

"The final war?" she asked, her voice dropping to a whisper.

"Armageddon!" Bob crowed. I stared into his scarred face as he grinned his insanity at me.

Stella clutched the top of her shirt. She seemed to struggle with the horror of it all before she swallowed hard and lifted her chin. "If God wishes to end the world," she said, "so be it!"

I growled at her. "I thought humility was one of the things your God wanted from you," I said. She shot me a questioning look, so I explained, "You are so damn arrogant. You are deciding on death for the entire world! You are trying to murder everyone!"

I realized I was wrong thinking my words would move her when I saw her jaw set.

"You think I'm playing God," she said. "But I'm just doing what God told me. And He isn't playing God, He is God."

Bob laughed in my face. "You can't stop us," he cackled. "We will win!"

Fenrir laughed along with him. "It will be a glorious ending!" he cried. "Come mortals! Free me, that I might do your god's bidding!"

The creature stretched his body, which seemed to writhe and grow in the magical firelight. The flames shot up to burn several feet high and crackled with blue sparks. I stared at him, realizing with horror that it wasn't an effect of the flickering light. The son of Loki was actually growing in size.

Bob took advantage of my distraction and shoved me away. I stumbled a moment, then recovered. I ran after him as he raced over to Stella. The woman startled, tearing her eyes away from Fenrir as Bob ran up to her. She fumbled with a chain around her neck.

Bob snarled wordlessly and pushed her hands away. He tore at her shirt and grabbed the chain, breaking it off of her neck. He ignored her cry of outrage, pushing her away. She fell back and kicked out, trying to move further away.

Bob laughed and turned towards the beast. I plowed into his back and the chain flew from his hands, landing several feet in front of the wolf.

Fenrir lunged to his feet, jaws snapping, his eyes fixed on the silver pendants glittering in the magical firelight. Stella screamed and ran back into the tunnels.

I grappled with Bob, each of us trying to get the other into a hold while struggling against being pinned. Bob got his arms wrapped around my right arm and wriggled his legs out from my attempt to lock my legs around them. I held his torso, keeping him from turning to flip me over by frogging my knees to either side.

A sudden pain shot through my arm as Bob sank his teeth into my flesh. I screamed with pain and rage and struck his back with my fist several times, releasing my hold on his waist.

Bob leveraged my movement to pull my arm around, using my weight to slide me from his back. I clawed at his shirt, trying to slow my fall from the slight advantage I'd had. My nails raked his shirt, dragging across it with a hiss of the fabric.

Despite my best efforts, Bob wrestled me onto my back. He straddled my waist and pinned me down, grinning like a madman at my struggles.

CHAPT 26

I tried to get my hands free from Bob's grasp. He chuckled pushing me back down. He leaned over, using his weight to hold me still.

"Poor, poor Nicola," he drawled. "Always fighting against the inevitable."

I smirked. "Tell me you aren't going to go all Agent Smith on me."

Bob smiled. "There you go, falling back on your sharp and wicked words." He dropped his head to whisper in my ear. "Did that help Keith in his last moments?"

I snarled and jerked under his grasp. "Bastard! Filthy piece of sh—"

"Hey now!" he snapped. "Watch your tongue, woman! 'Do not allow a woman to have authority over a man; instead, she is to be silent'; First Timothy 2:12."

I rolled my eyes. "Is that all you've got? Bad translations from a book written in a dead language by a bunch of fanatics intent on keeping women under their control?"

"It is as God decrees," he said. "If you read the Word of God, you would know that."

I rolled my eyes. "Why is it that when someone's trying to shove Christianity down my throat, they always assume I just completely missed the user manual? I've read the Bible, idiot! I wasn't impressed."

Bob frowned. "You didn't understand it—"

"Oh, sweet Frigga, give me patience!" I snapped. "I have a degree in literature, women's studies and psychology. The damn thing is written in English, with a million and one versions, six of which are on my bookshelf at home! It isn't that I don't understand it. I just don't agree with it."

I struggled to get up, knowing it wouldn't do any good, but unwilling to just lay there, helpless.

"Look, Bob," I muttered. "I'm glad you find it inspirational, or meaningful, or whatever, but I don't. I read it, and I see the bloody, oppressive history of the people who followed that book. I see the bigotry and hate corrupting the words of your God. And I'm sick and tired of people thinking that me not buying into the politics of the Nicean Council, or the misogyny of Paul, a man who got kicked in the head by a donkey and hallucinated. But he wrote a few damn letters telling people what to do, and you all take his words over Jesus. You know, the Christ. The guy your religion is named after!"

I took a deep breath and continued in a calmer voice. "It's not a matter of belief. Hell, I've even met your god, and if I wasn't sure before, I'm absolutely convinced now, because I will never bend a knee to someone who says giving people free will was the worst mistake he ever made."

Bob stared at me, his eye narrowed. "So, you are telling me that learning more about the Word of God would not move you to accepting Jesus?"

I stretched my neck up, raising my face closer to his. "It would not," I said, enunciating each word carefully.

A shadow fell over Bob's expression. "Then you are truly a sinner," he murmured. "You must be condemned to death."

I laughed. "Join or die, huh? Good plan," I said with as much sarcasm as I could muster. "Let's see how that works out for you."

Bob grinned again. "I will enjoy watching the beast make you his first victim," he said. "Do you suppose he will swallow you whole, or rip you apart first?"

"Never gonna happen, Bob," I said.

He just smiled. He grabbed the hair at the top of my head, still holding my wrists. He pulled me up, using both wrists and my hair as leverage.

I scrambled to my feet, gritting my teeth against the pain. Bob simply rolled his weight back onto his feet, pulling me up with him. He turned me so to face the rocky wall next to us, and my eyes went wide as I realized what he was going to do.

I tucked my chin as well as I could with Bob yanking my head back. The pain of the hair pulling at my scalp was sharp and made my eyes water. I squeezed them shut, scrunching my face up and bracing my feet against the ground.

Bob shoved wrists and head forward, hard. It seemed like forever before the impact. Pain exploded over my brow and nose, and I cried out. My face throbbed as my nose was ground into the stone.

The sharp sting on my scalp grabbed my attention, and I struggled against Bob's grasp as he drove my head forward again. This time, I hit the rock with mostly my forehead. The blow made me stagger, losing the little bit of leverage I had. The third time, I managed to turn my head slightly, taking the impact on my cheek. I could feel the rough stone cutting into my flesh.

I could feel my consciousness pulling away from the beating, and I let it happen. It wouldn't be the first time I'd escaped the pain of what was happening to me in that way.

In some ways, it seemed like that was all that ever happened to me. My time at home, being a mother and a businesswoman, was just a brief intermission between these sessions of people trying to hurt me, trying to kill me... or worse.

They were always taking away my bodily autonomy, doing things to me, breaking my flesh or my will. It was frustrating and infuriating, and I couldn't seem to find a way to make it stop. I couldn't force them to leave me be. I supposed I could just let them get away with whatever they were doing.

Keith could have started his little army for Armageddon. Zaro could have kept violating women and children, while Nancy continued to abuse the Healing Rune by withholding it from those who couldn't pay hundreds or thousands of dollars.

And then there was Bob. Always trying to do the will of Jehovah... or was it Satan? Did it matter? Whoever it was Bob got marching orders from took advantage of the man's rabid faith to forward their own apocalyptic ending. And good ol' Bob just kept showing up, determined to destroy this world.

But I live here. And Ella and Maria lived here. My mother, Joseph, if he was even still alive. Hound Dog and Ames. All of my friends, my kith and kin, would literally end if I let it happen. How could I ever give up on stopping that?

I couldn't, and that was the answer. I felt blood and sweat cooling on my face as the strange, hot fullness crept up my neck and ears. My anger this time wasn't about what happened to me. What happened to me was where my fear came from. My anger, my rage, my righteous wrath, that came from my love of the people in my life. I didn't try to stop these people to save myself.

Tyr had said it as it was, warriors didn't make it out. I was saving my daughters. I was saving my friends. I was saving the laughter and the hugs. I was saving long conversations over coffee and helping homeless kids find their place in the world. I was saving an honest but surly detective who managed to do the right thing even when it was confusing as hell.

My face stopped hitting the wall. At some point, I had fallen to my knees. I struggled for breath through a broken, swelling nose, keeping my eyes shut. I felt something wet bubble out of one nostril, then pop. I let myself sag to one side. Pain shot through my head and I groaned softly. The sound vibrated through my skull, and I regretted making the noise.

Bob shoved me forward, releasing my hands and my hair. I caught myself on the rock, barely keeping myself from sliding all the way to the ground.

Bob's feet crunched on the loose dirt and pebbles on the surface of the ground. By the sound of it, he was moving away. I turned my head and cracked open one eye. It was swelling, but I forced it to open enough to see by.

Bob was walking away, moving towards Fenrir. His arms spread wide as if he was walking to some kind of reward, some honoring of his deeds. I guessed that was about what he was feeling about the situation. He knew he'd won. He'd beaten me, and now he was free to complete the task he'd been given.

Only he didn't know that beating me wasn't enough.

I pressed my hands against the wall, forcing myself up. I swallowed a groan of pain and focused my attention on the man walking towards the beast.

Fenrir stood on all four feet and stared at the man, focused completely on his desire to be freed and the one who would do that. He strained at his bonds like a dog on a leash.

I let the warm lava flowing into my head take over. My vision washed with yellow once more, and I found that the Berserking effect seemed to counter the pain and swelling in my nose and eyes. I reached up and wiped my upper lip with the back of my hand. I glanced down to see the red liquid glistening against my skin.

My tongue touched the blood on my lip, and the rage howled at the taste. I couldn't tell if it was pleasure at the blood or rage at the injury. I didn't really care though. I gritted my teeth as I forced my feet to move, wincing at the two molars that shot pain through my jaw.

I let the Eleventh Runespell guide my body. I embraced the rage and let it wash over me in a way that I hadn't done since I'd beaten Zaro into a coma. Once again, my baby's life was at stake, and I was not about to let that go unanswered.

The Berserker within, the cat spirit that gave me my rage, took hold of my limbs. I stalked across the ground, silently. A strange feeling of being unseen washed over me. I watched the wolf-creature for any sign that he had spotted my movement, but his eyes remained locked on Bob.

I moved closer, only a few feet away. Something in my gut told me that moving too quickly would break whatever magic kept the creature from noticing me.

The man stopped in front of the pendants lying in the dirt. He raised his hands, palm up.

"Great monster," he intoned. "You are surely one of the beasts of the Book of Revelations. Your release will be a sign of the power of God and the truth of His Word."

The beast pulled at his chains again. "Hurry, mortal," he huffed impatiently. "Lest someone else try to foil your plans."

Bob lowered his hands, making a show of not rushing. I moved up behind the man, grinning at Bob's need to ritualize the whole thing. The wolf still staring at him as he lowered himself to one knee to pick up the pendants.

Bob raised the chain in both hands, showing the wolf the silver runes. "Look, beast! The key to your freedom. As it is said in Psalms 107:14, 'He brought them out of darkness and gloom and broke their chains apart.' So shall the Lord break the chains that bind you here!"

I reached over Bob's head and snatched the chain and pendants out of his hands.

CHAPT 27

Without waiting for a reaction from either beast or man, I turned and ran for the tunnels, slapping the handful of metal at the silver cord around my neck. I willed the pendants to attach to the strand of Gleipnir as the thudding of my feet on the rock floor pounded in my aching head.

Bob crashed into my back a moment later, sending us careening into the wall. The thin chain that Stella had worn flew from my fingers, and Bob scrambled after it.

I sat up and checked my own chain, smiling when I confirmed what I already knew. There were seven pendants attached to the silver strand. The irony of my necklace didn't escape me. It was a small portion of the chain that bound the creature only a few yards away.

"No!" Bob cried. He whipped around to glare at me, rage distorting his features and pulling at the scars on his face unnaturally. "Where are they? What did you do to them?"

I grinned, showing my teeth through battered lips. "I've collected them," I said. "That's what I do."

His eyes jumped to my chest where the chain with its many charms was now visible. He lunged at me with a wordless cry. My yellow vision saw clearly, so that it seemed like his movements slowed just enough for me to keep up with them, to plan my reaction with the help of the sigil on my chest.

I pushed up to my knees and struck out with my fist. The blow connected with his jaw. The impact turned him sideways, and he barely missed tackling me. Instead, he brushed past my shoulder, nearly knocking me over.

I got to my feet as he turned, his fist flying at me. The pendant burned against my chest and I ducked under his arm, somersaulting under the blow and back onto my feet.

Bob came at me again, this time more controlled. I remembered thinking that he'd been ex-military when I'd first seen him a few years ago, and his posture now spoke of hand to hand combat training. He hunched over, making his body into a smaller target, holding his arms close to his body. I smirked as I crouched down, mimicking his posture.

Bob threw an open-handed blow at my head. I moved just enough for him to miss me and returned with a jab at his chest. He shifted back, turning slightly, and used the motion for another strike. I dodged that and moved backwards a step. He stepped forward, as well, keeping the distance between us constant.

Bob threw another open-handed blow, and I blocked it with my arm, sending an underhanded jab with my other hand into his abdomen. I could feel the muscles tensed under the impact and I realized, too late, that he'd drawn me in.

I dropped back, but Bob's other hand was already at my neck. He grabbed my hair and reached for the chain. I bent my fingers, holding them like claws, and raked at his face. He flinched back, roaring with pain and anger. Red lines, too thin to be from normal human nails, appeared on his cheeks in the wake of my fingers.

He cocked his free hand and sent a punch at my face. I thrust up my hands, only just barely catching and deflecting the blow upwards so it grazed my scalp instead of plowing into my already broken nose.

Bob brought his hand down, and I shoved it to the side, the momentum causing both of us to turn. He used the movement to try to wrap his arm around my neck from behind. I twisted, jabbing my elbows back in alternating thrusts against his torso. He grunted several times with the blows and loosened his hold.

I dropped into a partial squat and elbowed him in the groin. He let out an 'oof' and a groan, telling me my aim had been true. I shifted my weight to lunge forward away from him, but a sudden sharp pressure at my throat brought me up short. Bob had grabbed the chain around my neck.

Though it appeared to be a delicate silver strand, the magical necklace could never break or be removed from my neck without my consent. Bob obviously didn't know that, because he kept pulling at it, turning the necklace into a garrote.

I gagged and struggled under the pressure for a moment before I got my legs under me and stood up. The pressure on my throat lessened, and I managed to take a breath before he tightened his grip and pulled again.

I pulled my head forward, straining and pulling against the sharp, cutting pressure of the chain, then I whipped my head back, letting his efforts add to the momentum. I heard the crunch of bone as the back of my skull hit him in the face. I hoped I'd broken his nose, turn about being fair play and all.

The impact must have jarred him pretty well, at least. The necklace went slack around my neck, and I lunged forward. He still had a hold of the chain, but it only dug painfully into my throat for a second before I was free.

I spun around to face him. "You can't take this chain off of me, Bob," I sneered. "It's the same stuff that keeps the doggo over there out of the neighbor's yard."

Bob's eyes flickered down to the necklace before returning to my face. "Then, I'll use the pendant to release it," he snapped.

I barked a hoarse laugh at him. "It can't be removed except by my will."

The man frowned. "Demon magic!"

"Something you would know about, huh?" I retorted, reminding him of the monsters he'd commanded a few years ago. "Didn't save you back then, though, did it?"

Bob's eyes narrowed. "Magic often ends with death," he pointed out. "I guess I'll just have to cut your bitch head off."

"You can try," I snarled.

Bob lunged forward with a series of rapid attacks that I could barely follow, consciously. I dropped into the stance for the kata Rade had taught me and went through the blocks in rapid succession. He landed a blow on my shoulder, though he'd been aiming for my chest. The impact drove me back two steps, but I shifted my feet and kept my balance, ready to block his next attack.

Instead, he began circling me. Rade had said that movement could hide the telegraphing of attacks. I let my consciousness unfocus, pulling the energy of the cat spirit to the fore once again.

Bob feinted twice and, though I crouched to brace myself each time, I didn't give him the opening he'd been going for. The third time, he attacked for real with a rapid double punch.

I blocked the lower first one to the side, but dropped to one knee under the second, aimed for my face. Before my knee hit the ground, I lashed out with my own punch, hitting him just below the waist at the bladder with the heel of my hand. It was a hard hit, and the sharp, acrid smell of urine filled the cavern.

Bob groaned again, bending over. He shuffled backwards away from me. I got back to my feet and moved towards him. I grabbed his head and slammed it down, bringing my knee up into his face. Bob dropped to his knees in front of me, and I punched him in the face. I hit him again, then a third time. Blood sprayed across my face, and I took a handful of his hair, pulling his head up.

"Why won't you just die?" he snarled, slurring his words with the blood pooling at the corners of his mouth. "Just die already."

I grinned in his face. "Oh, Bob," I said. "I feel the same way about you."

I pulled back and punched him once more. I felt the crack of his cheekbone breaking under my fist. He fell at my feet and lay still. I stared down at him, hate and glee, satisfaction and fear, all filling my gut. Part of me wanted to beat him more, part wanted to flee. There was even a small thread of sympathy for the man who had struggled so hard to destroy me.

The emotion that won the battle deep inside would dictate the final course of action I would take, but until then, I just watched him bleed. As my mind pulled back from the immediate focus of combat, I could hear an odd sound. The deep, huffing laughter of the son of Loki echoed through the silence.

I glanced over at the beast, amazed that I could have forgotten the monster was still there.

"What's so funny?" I asked. "I won. You will stay trapped here forever."

"Not forever," he chuckled. "Just until the end of time, at least for the Nine Worlds."

"Close enough," I muttered.

"Unless..."

I turned to face the creature. "Unless what?"

"Unless you would free me," he said.

"Why would I ever do that?"

Fenrir circled around before sitting, just like I'd seen dogs do. "Because you can't be sure what kind of creature I am," he said.

"Oh, yes, I can," I snarled. "The prophecy—"

"The prophecy has an agenda," the wolf snapped. "And I'm sure you are aware of how many such predictions end up coming to pass because of the fears surrounding what was predicted."

I huffed. "Yeah," I muttered. "Self-fulfilling prophecies. I'm familiar with those."

Fenrir cocked his head to one side, his too-short ears swiveling forward. "Self-fulfilling prophecy. I like that," he murmured to himself before refocusing on me. "You don't know that I would have wrought destruction had I not been chained."

I shrugged. "Maybe," I admitted. "But there was a chance."

The wolf snorted. "I was judged by the fears of the Æsir, the cowardly gods, not by my own Örlog!"

I considered his words. He was technically right. Örlog was a person's reputation, the kind of person they were, from how honest to how hard working they were, and everything in between. It could be changed by changing their behavior or by making a grievous mistake. Even the kinds of friends they made and associated with, and the family they were born to or raised by could affect their Örlog.

Fenrir was born of Loki, the trickster god and often the scapegoat of the Æsir. It wasn't that Loki didn't deserve a lot of the blame that came his way, but he certainly didn't get any benefit of the doubt. That deep-seated distrust had trickled down to all of Loki's children.

On the other hand, Fenrir had been raised in Asgard by the Æsir. Everything he was at his birth had been shaped by the gods, particularly Tyr, who had been the closest to the wolf as he grew. Tyr knew Fenrir better than anyone in all the Nine Worlds, and probably beyond that. Tyr had been the closest thing to a friend and father that the wolf had ever known.

Yet, when it came time to make the choice, Tyr had sacrificed his own honor, risked his own Örlog, given up his own limb, to bind Fenrir in this place.

When all was said and done, I couldn't think of a reason to believe that Tyr hadn't had a basis for his decision. I knew there was a chance that I was wrong, and that it was possible that Tyr had been wrong. But that was the risk of making a choice with no clear answer.

I looked up at the wolf who had watched me closely as I thought about his situation. He seemed to be smiling as if he could see the doubt in my mind.

"You have a point, Fenrir, son of Loki," I said, choosing my words carefully. "But you are Odinslayer. You are the Bound One. Even the god of honor and justice was willing to use falsehoods to protect the Nine Worlds from your nature and your bloodlust. I have no reason to counter that act."

Fenrir leaped to his feet. His ears pulled back against his head, and his lips pulled back from his too-large teeth. "Coward!"

I shook my head. "I cannot think that I would know your nature better than those who lived with you for so long," I said. "Once I say, I will not free you."

Fenrir lunged forward, snapping his jaws at me. The chain brought him up short long before he could reach me. "You cannot keep me here," he snarled. "I have done nothing to deserve this!"

I took a deep shuddering breath. "Twice I say," I continued. "I will not free you."

The wolf sat back on his haunches and howled. The sound filled the cave, echoing off the walls and down the tunnels. It was so loud it made my ears ring, and so mournful I nearly wept.

I shook my head to clear it as the sound faded away. I looked back up at the beast. My eyes felt full and heavy with unshed tears, though it might have just been the multiple blows to the face. "Thrice I say, so know it to be true," I said. "I. Will not. Free you."

Fenrir stared at me for a long time. I raised my chin, showing my resolve. Then he dropped his head, dejectedly, his shoulders shaking with sobs that were almost silent after the howls just moments before.

I let my shoulders slump. In a lot of ways I could feel his pain. He'd been trapped by circumstance as much as I had, and we had both had to live with a constant suffering because of what others had done to us.

I nearly reached out to him, but I only took a single step forward when he raised his head. His mouth was pulled into a wolfish smile, and I realized he hadn't been crying. My stomach lurched with fear. He'd been laughing.

I frowned. "Why do you laugh?" I asked. "I just told you I would not free you."

"Yes, hero of the Runespells," the beast said. "And now you will die!"

A gunshot echoed through the cavern, cutting through the sound of Fenrir's laughter.

CHAPT 28

"Learn to carve them, learn to read them, learn to stain them, learn to validate them, learn to summon them, learn to modify them, learn to share them, learn to use them."

Time stopped for a moment as I raced through the cavern. The Runespells had touched my skin and the familiar chant, the words of the Hávamál spoken in the voice of Odin, the Allfather, had rung in my ears in the eternity between two heartbeats.

"I have learned the fourth spell: Whether bound by hand or bound by feet, or bound by anything, a touch and a word is all that is needed to break the chains that bind."

I had understood the meaning of the Fourth Runespell, and all its possibilities, as the words rang in my head. If I could have breathed, I would have gasped at the knowledge.

Before I could even blink, before the last echoes of the fourth Runespell had faded, the words of the Fifth Runespell pulsed with the chanting rhythm in my mind.

"I have learned the fifth spell: When weapons that fly through the air would threaten myself or my kith or kin, my will and desire alone is enough to prevent any injury from it, so long as I know that the threat is there."

•　　•　　•

I blinked up at the wolf as several more shots rang out. He continued to laugh for a moment, then he stopped short and stared at me with a confused expression.

"You did not die," he murmured.

I thought I detected a note of awe in his voice, but I dismissed it to focus on something far more pressing. I turned to find Bob on his knees, leaning against the wall. His mouth hung open as he stared at me. He held the gun in both hands, the tip drooping down as his grip weakened.

"Oh, dear Bob," I said, shaking my head at him. "So close, but not quite."

His face took on a panicked expression as I walked towards him with a measured pace.

I tsked at him. "You focused so much on the pendant to free Fenrir that you forgot about the other one." I crouched down in front of him, and gently but firmly took the gun from his hands.

"The other one?" he croaked.

"The other Runespell, Bob," I said in a stage whisper.

"No!" Fenrir roared behind us. "You have the Fifth Runespell, too!"

I glanced back at the beast, then turned and smiled at Bob. "The pendant that you knew" - I poked his arm in time to "you knew" - "would protect Stella when you shot at her and Joseph."

I leaned forward. "Now I know how the Runespell works, I know what you both did," I said. "She could have chosen to save Joseph, too, couldn't she?"

Bob curled his lip in a snarl.

"But she didn't," I said. "And I hate her for that. And I hate you for pulling the trigger, Bob."

I stood up and took a step back. I watched the man thoughtfully as he cowered against the wall. Finally, I turned sideways and stood tall, my back straight. I stretched my arm up, holding the gun straight above my head, then I lowered it slowly until it pointed at his scarred temple.

"I'm tired, Bob," I said, quietly, without any heat or anger in my voice. "I'm tired of fighting with you, over and over again. I'm tired of your face, poking up every time I turn around, causing death and pain wherever you go."

Bob's eyes flicked to the gun, then back to my face.

I sighed. "I said I wouldn't do it, Bob." I watched his posture relax. "I said I wouldn't be afraid to pull the trigger, that I wouldn't play this game of fighting the same people over and over."

Bob's eyes widened. He started gibbering, protests spilling out faster than his scarred and swollen lips could form.

"I'm not playing anymore, Bob," I said, my voice rising over his pleas. "This game is over."

The gun roared as my finger tightened on the trigger. I squeezed again, then again and again until the roaring stopped.

I stared at the lump of clothes and flesh lying at my feet. I couldn't tell if the sound of the gunshots had caused temporary deafness or if the cavern was just that silent. A dark pool spread out from the lump. I watched it grow, both fascinated and horrified by what I'd done.

Part of me drooled over the power of death that I had wielded. It craved the rush of taking life again. But it was different from the Berserker. The spiritual rage didn't kill for the power of it. It lusted after the physical battles, hot and sweaty and bodies against bodies with metal and wood only to enhance what the person was. This was a cold and distant and dry, with no effort and too much power over others. I rolled the feeling around in my mind, tasting it, comparing it to the alive feel of Berserking.

I didn't like it.

I bent down to check for a pulse. The skull had broken off into several pieces. Apparently, human heads weren't built to take several point-blank shots. Satisfied that the body wouldn't rise to attack me again, I dropped the empty gun beside it.

I barely noticed that the hand that had held the gun tingled from the vibrations of the shots. I didn't think about how rhythmically I rubbed my hand against my thigh, my fingers making an inaudible da-da-da-da, da-da-da-da as they bumped over the seam of my pants.

I turned back to the wolf. I wasn't sure why, but I needed to see that he was still there. Perhaps it was the remote, surreal way my body felt like the real me was just a bit out of alignment with my physical self. But I needed to see another being. I needed to know that reality had still kept going.

I wanted to know that I hadn't failed by making the choice to kill… him.

Fenrir stared at me, unmoving. He seemed as shocked by my actions as I was. Despite the fact that the wolf had distracted me several times, I had beaten him. But I wasn't sure he hadn't beaten me, too.

I realized what had really happened. Here, deep in this cave, with no witnesses, I could get away with murder and no one would know. No one had seen it except for the giant mythological beast. I wouldn't be held accountable even if the gods knew what happened. I didn't have to face what I'd done to… him.

Then I knew what I had to do. For myself, for my kids, for the sake of the whole damn quest and the title of "hero." I could pretend the whole thing hadn't happened, and the stain of hiding it would blacken me more than anything else I could do.

"Bob," I choked out.

Fenrir's ears swung forward. He started as if he was going to move, but he stayed where he was, still watching me with wide, yellow-red eyes.

"His name was Bob," I said again. "I killed him, and I can't just... not say his name."

The beast shifted his head slightly as if he wanted to turn away from me but didn't dare.

"I own what I have done," I said, my voice high-pitched with the panic and hysteria that I could feel just behind my eyes. "I killed Bob. And I stopped him from freeing you, son of Loki."

Fenrir dropped his head a few inches. I got the feeling he was trying to figure out what to do. His expression was so confused, like he had never seen someone die. But he had spent the last however long I'd been in this deep dark cavern begging to be freed so he could go on a killing rampage.

The more I watched him and thought about it, the more I was convinced this was Fenrir's first real encounter with violent death. The idea struck me as hilarious, and I started laughing.

The beast dropped down, laying in a submissive posture. This made me laugh even harder.

"I'm not afraid of the big bad wolf," I cried. "The big bad wolf is afraid of me."

Somewhere in my laughter, the tears began. I wept hard, sobbing over the stress, the pressure, the frustrations. I cried over Stella and whatever in her life had driven her to become who she was. I cried over Fenrir and the creature he might have been before the stupid prophecy interrupted his life.

I cried over Bob, and his stupid death, and I cried over my own lost bit of innocence that killing him had cost me. I cried over Joseph, my dear friend, who was lying outside the cave, cold and alone, dead or dying with no one there to comfort him...

Joseph.

"I'm coming, Joseph," I muttered, dashing the tears from my eyes as I stood up from where I'd fallen to my knees.

"Don't leave me," the wolf whined from behind me. "Don't leave me alone."

I turned back to the creature. I couldn't help but sympathize with him.

"You've been alone for centuries," I pointed out. "It'll be just like before."

"I know," he said, his head hanging down.

"I have a friend I need to get back to," I said, trying to explain. "Maybe, once I make sure he's okay, I can... I don't know, bring you something?"

"Something? I want only my freedom. What could you bring me that would substitute?"

I shrugged. "I don't know." I considered my earlier thoughts. "What do you eat down here?"

"The bodies of the dead."

I jumped at the sound of the quiet but firm female voice coming from behind me. Fenrir jumped to his feet, his tail actually wagging with happiness.

I turned to face whoever had come this time. Whatever I expected, it was nothing like what I found when I turned around.

A woman appeared, stepping out of the shadows. But she remained a part of the shadows. Her skin was ebony, like charred carcasses, and ivory, like the flesh of a new corpse. Each color flowed around the other, constantly moving across her skin like a kaleidoscope of light and shadow.

Where the black stayed for more than an instant, the flesh began to peel back as if burned or rotted away, exposing muscle and bone underneath it. When the white flowed where the flesh was gone, it grew back, writhing like maggots.

Despite the horror of her ever transforming skin, the woman was beautiful. Her hair fell in lush inky black locks that transformed into white spider silk. Her eyes were dark pools of sorrow. Simply looking into them drained all hope and desire to live from my soul.

I blinked and looked away from them, focusing on her mouth instead.

"Hel," I croaked.

CHAPT 29

The woman inclined her head. "Indeed," she said. Her voice was soothing, a balm to a battered soul, stripping away any thoughts of resisting her. Her voice promised rest from the never-ending rush and pain and work of life, offering peace... but not forgiveness.

She stepped toward Bob's body. I watched with morbid curiosity as she moved her hands over it. A wisp of something like smoke or steam drifted out from the dead flesh.

"What was that?" I asked.

Hel glanced at me. "His essence," she said. "His soul, you might call it."

I swallowed. "Is he in Helheim, then? Did you claim him?"

"No," she said in a matter-of-fact tone. She bent down to grab the corpse by the waistband of his pants. "His beliefs prevent me from claiming him." She stood up, hefting Bob's body with one hand.

"Then why are you here?" I asked. "If you aren't collecting one of your souls... What are you doing with him?"

Hel's lips curved into a beautiful smile, and it was terrifying to see. "I'm here to feed my brother," she said.

She carried the body over to the wolf-creature and tossed it to him. Fenrir caught it the way a dog catches kibble in mid-air, snapping his jaws around it. He raised his muzzle, stretching out his neck and I stared as a lump moved down his throat.

Bile pushed at the back of my throat, and I swallowed several times to keep it down. "He eats people?" I said, my voice cracking.

Hel laughed, a melodious tinkling sound that brought to mind the screams of the dying. "As I said before, he eats the bodies of the dead," she said. "Normally I bring him some, but why should I haul corpses when you were kind enough to provide one."

I couldn't keep the look of horrified disgust off my face.

"Don't be like that," she chided. "You act as though you don't know what kind of beings we are." She gestured at the beast. "My brother and I are true to ourselves. We are the children of Jötun. We are as far from being human as can be while still keeping the form."

I looked at Fenrir, then back at her. My eyebrows rose.

Hel shrugged. "Well, I keep a semblance of the form, at least," she conceded.

"Is that why the Norns wanted to stop you?" I asked. "To keep you from harvesting more... corpses?" I immediately regretted asking the question. Really, the last thing I wanted was to continue this interaction.

Hel looked at me as if studying a bug she'd found. "Is that what they told you?" she asked.

I nodded.

She shook her head. "I have enough souls, dear child. A few more here and there wouldn't make much difference to me." She smiled again, sending shivers across my skin. "My due will come to me in the end, regardless."

"So you didn't threaten to kill people?" I asked.

"How could I?" she asked. "As a god-creature, I am forbidden from interfering with human choices."

I bit my lip. The Norns had lied to me. In retrospect, I hadn't demanded they speak the truth to me, and they had lied to get me to do exactly what they wanted. It was my own fault for taking such beings at face value. Still, I wondered if they had lied to me about there being a person born to use the Second Runespell, the Healing rune.

"So you visit Fenrir and feed him corpses?" I asked. "That's... nice of you."

Hel shrugged. "He must eat to grow," she said. "And he must grow so that he might eventually break Gleipnir and play his part in the Great Battle."

"Yeah, you must be thrilled about that," I said. "You get to help destroy the world."

She stared at me. I looked away from those horrible sad eyes.

"We all do our duty," she said. "Yours is to delay the Great Battle. Mine is to contribute to it, when it comes."

I shrugged. "I guess."

"Do you not believe in the cycles of life?" she asked. "Do you not walk the völva path?"

I blinked. The völva were powerful women in old Norse cultures. They were feared for the magic they could do and respected for the knowledge and wisdom they could bring. To be a völva was to achieve a significant place in Norse society.

"I-I guess," I said. "I mean, I do believe in the cycles."

"How can the world be renewed if it is not destroyed first?" she asked. "Do not hate the dry rot that breaks down the trunks of the tallest trees. For they make room for the saplings struggling beneath the towering branches."

I nodded. "I know," I said. "It's just harder to accept when it's your whole existence that's dry-rotting."

Hel nodded. "Just as the grub feels when the log it lives under breaks away."

I sucked on my teeth, thinking about the truth of that.

She stared into the distance. "You have a friend who needs you," she reminded me. "There is nothing more for you here."

"Oh, Joseph!" I backed away from the children of Loki for several steps, then turned and ran for the tunnels. I made it two whole steps before my body started protesting with all the injuries and bruises I'd gotten from my fight with Bob.

I hobbled and lurched through the tunnels, but I only made it around the first bend before I had to pause and take stock of my injuries. Leaning against the wall, I tried not to pant too loudly. I heard a faint growling, then Hel's voice drifted from behind me. "Don't be foolish, you old Garmr, you silly old rag. Why would I tell her about the gate? I'd never have peace and quiet again!"

I shook my head. Now was not the time to deal with more godly riddles. I pushed away from the wall and limped through the darkness, barely able to pull up the Berserker enough to give me night vision. It took ten times as long, and six pit stops to get to the mouth of the cave even though I didn't have to stop and get my ass kicked as I had on the way in.

I gasped with relief when I saw the starlight at the mouth, and I staggered out from under the curtain of roots into a scene of absolute chaos. People rushed back and forth, carrying bags and cases. It took me a moment to realize most of them were EMTs and park rangers. Three of them brushed past me before a fourth stopped and peered at my face.

I blinked in shock at her before she turned and yelled at a few guys nearby, and I was soon seated with my back against the rocky hillside with three people gently prodding at my face and hands. I was proclaimed to have a broken nose, two broken fingers, a chipped tooth, and a several bruised and broken ribs.

"Let's get her in the ambulance with the other one, then we can look for the missing one," the woman EMT said. She looked at me with a mixture of admiration and concern. "I don't know how you are still upright."

She started to move away before I realized what she'd said.

"Wait," I cried. "The other one? And a missing one?"

The woman paused and nodded. "Yeah, that's why we're here. We got a call that some guy got shot. Found him over there." She gestured towards where we'd set up the tent hours before.

"Is he-?" I swallowed, staring at her intently so I wouldn't look in the direction she'd pointed. I didn't think I could handle the memories right now.

The woman stared at me for a moment, then her face relaxed into a smile. "No, hon," she said. "He's still fighting. We got here just in time, I think."

I sighed, relieved that Joseph still had a chance. "What did you say about someone missing?"

The woman frowned. "There was a woman who came out of the cave before you. Said you were fighting with another guy."

I frowned. I'd nearly forgotten about Stella. "Is she...?"

"Taken into custody," she assured me. "It's a good thing your guides called us. Between the three of you, arresting the woman, and this missing guy... You know you aren't supposed to apprehend an escaped convict. That's the cops' job." She shook her head.

I grimaced. "Yeah, I gue-Wait. Our guides?" I asked, wondering who she might be talking about.

The woman nodded towards the campsite, and I finally looked in the direction she indicated. Rade was bent over, picking up pieces of trash after the EMTs. Her face was drawn into a scowl. As I watched, her head snapped up and she stood, stalking over to a young park ranger. I couldn't hear what she said to the kid, but he turned three shades of red and nearly bowed to her before running off.

Nearby, Mercy was squatting down near where the tent had been set up. She chatted with an EMT while shoving cooking equipment into my discarded pack. The tent seemed to already have been packed up.

"Mercy! Rade!" I croaked out, wincing at the pain shooting through my side at the effort.

The two looked up and rushed over to me. I wondered how I would be able to communicate what had happened with all the people around. The woman EMT touched my shoulder to get my attention and helped me lay back on a stretcher that two others had laid out beside me.

Mercy dropped down at my side and grabbed my hand. "Nicola, what happened?"

I squeezed her hand back and winced as pain shot through my fingers. "He was gunned down by his own arrogance," I said, enunciating the words in what I hoped was a meaningful way. "I hope he's in hell." My head fell back as more pain shot through my body as the last dregs of the pain-numbing adrenaline left me.

"You stopped him?" Rade asked.

I grimaced. "He's dog food."

I watched the two Valkyrie scowl, then Mercy's face brightened. She opened her mouth as if to speak, but shot a glance at the EMTs surrounding me and snapped her jaw shut. I winked at her.

She patted my leg and the woman EMT told a pair of men to take me up to the trail. After several minutes of them puffing their way up the winding path with me riding the stretcher like it was a ship on a stormy sea, we reached the main trail.

The guys attached my stretcher to a three-wheeled ATV that was waiting at the top, and I was soon speeding down the bumpy trail to the nearest access point. Within a half-hour, I was strapped into the ambulance next to Joseph. He was unconscious, but the EMT in the ambulance said he was stable.

After a moment of staring at him, trying to reassure myself that he would be okay, I lay my head back and slept.

CHAPT 30

I watched Ella and Maria piled up on the same camping chair, whispering over the laptop in their combined laps. They had found some new music program or video game, and they spent a lot of time discussing the details of it as if it were some lost treasure that no one could know about.

I smiled and stretched my feet out under the table towards the fire pit on the other side. My ribs twinged with a faint pain left over from my physical injuries. I stared into the flames for a long moment, letting the fire entrance me.

The sliding door opened, and Joseph came out carrying a platter of sliced salami, cheeses and crackers. He was animated, talking to my mother about a TV show that they both loved. He winked at me as he set the platter down on the table in front of me and took the chair to my left.

My mother sat down her plate of veggies and dips and sat in the chair on my right. She smiled at me before continuing her conversation with Joseph. I let the pleasant, comforting mood wash over me as I took a pull from the bottle of hard cider in my hand.

It had all worked out, as usual. Joseph had spent a week in the hospital, and another few weeks recovering at home. I'd gotten back home around the same time, with orders to wrap my torso each day to support the injured ribs.

Stella was back in prison, though I wasn't sure how I felt about that. I had believed her when she said she hadn't done anything to deserve her sentence, but she had also tried to destroy the world, so there was that.

No one seemed to be too worried that Bob had disappeared. I'd told Mercy and Joseph what had happened in the cave. They had gotten very quiet when I told them I'd killed Bob. Now Joseph was slowly coming back to being able to be around me without just staring at me with a pensive look of pain mixed with sorrow.

Mercy had just frowned and nodded, like it was something she had expected but didn't approve of. That had hurt more than I'd thought it would.

I had considered talking to Ames, thinking he would be able to understand the hard choices, but he seemed busy with his new position, and I didn't want to waste his time without knowing for sure if he would turn around and arrest me for murder. He was a stickler for the rules a bit too much for me to be able to guess his reaction.

Joseph's voice rose as he quoted some lines in a funny voice. My mother laughed at that and shot back with a responding quote. I smiled at them and glanced over at the girls, giggling and whispering between themselves.

I let my head fall back, and I stared up into the night sky. My throat felt full and my eyes stung with tears. No matter what happened to me, no matter what fresh hell or torture awaited me next time, I had this right here. I had my friends, my family, good food, warm fire, and a night under the stars, all still here because of me.

Sure, I had nightmares. Yeah, I was paying out the nose for Dr. Walters. I wasn't sure I'd ever get a decent rate on my insurance with how often I was in the hospital these days, but these people here were safe and alive.

And that was why I could keep going.

ABOUT THE AUTHOR

Sarah is an AuthorGoddess, one who embraces the divine honor of creating worlds with words in the hope of inspiring others. Sarah has been writing for more than 25 years, starting with poetry before moving on to non-fiction and fiction. She lives in the Midwest with two monsters (the kids), an ogre (the hubby), and whatever drama-llama is coming to visit this week.

Sarah is the author of *Too Wyrd* and *Fluffy Bunny*, books 1 & 2 of *The Runespells Series*. She has short stories and essays in several anthologies, including *Counterclockwise: A Time Travel Anthology*, *A Twist of Fate: A Collection of 11 Twisted Fairy Tales*, and *Whispers of Hope: A Lexis Infinitum Charity Anthology*. Sarah also writes on her blog, *The Author Goddess*, and makes funny videos about writing on her vlog, *Practically Writing*.

Thank you so much for reading one of our **Fantasy** novels.
If you enjoyed our book, please check out our recommended title for your
next great read!

War of the Staffs by Steve Stephenson & K.M. Tedrick

"Offers an enjoyable romp for high fantasy fans." *–KIRKUS REVIEWS*

View other Black Rose Writing titles at www.blackrosewriting.com/books

and use promo code **PRINT** to receive a **20% discount** when purchasing